Chicana Paradise
and Other Stories

by

Jesi Lopez Malignaggi

First Edition, January 2020

ISBN: 978-0-578-63493-7

Published in the United States of America by Trias Press in 2020

Edited & Book Design by Daniel J. Malignaggi

To my family

Table of Contents

Prologue

Luna

"Let me out! Let me out! Please...someone! Anyone...let me out!" She pounded the door until her small knuckles on her soft fingers bled. She kicked the door furiously until her bare toes ached. She had felt the door scrape her face as she slid down to the floor of the dark and cavernous closet. She began to whimper like a newborn puppy looking for her mother to suckle on. Luna knew no one would come to her rescue. No one. Even so, she continued to plea as she tasted her snot and salty tears ooze into her mouth.

The old women had warned her that if she did not do her daily chores, or if she caused any disturbance, there would be a penalty to pay. She might have scorched a table napkin when she was ironing earlier or had wasted too much time at the outside water pump filling the pitcher that morning. The old woman watched everything and began to add up insignificant slips-ups while grumbling under her breath. The tiny girl had been scrubbing yet another load of wash in the metal tub that was much too big to manage, which caused her back to throb throughout the morning from her bent awkward position.

Six-year-old Luna had been balancing herself on an old crate on the tips of her tiny toes so she could reach over and pull the old woman's clothes and linens from the scalding water and scrub them on a worn wooden washboard that was too wide to steady in the soapy liquid. The woman had been glaring at her all morning long from across the room. She was waiting for an excuse to beat the child. The old woman continued to curse and mumble as she stepped into the washroom. She stared at Luna, and then at once, yanked her off her toes and gave her a beating.

After pounding on the small child, the woman dragged her by her tiny soft arm. Luna was dazed from the beating and started to moan. She felt her body being pulled from the floor that she scrubbed earlier, to the kitchen doorway and on to the front porch, where her legs got scraped on the old creaky boards she swept the day before. Her whole body ached. She went limp for an instant, but then at the same time, something happened to her. She felt a surge of strength fill her entire body. It came from somewhere deep inside. She began to scream, kick, and cry out. The old woman did not flinch one bit. She just screamed at her to "Shut-up!" and grasped her tighter. The tugging and dragging continued from the porch down the one wooden step and across the dirt yard to the barn as the chickens scattered, squawking and shrieking about trying to get away from the abusive scene. The girl thrashed and implored mercy from the old woman, but she was deaf to it.

The yelling and cussing continued as Luna was lugged into the barn. The woman was strong as she towed the child to the very back of the barn where there was a door. She pulled the young girl close to her. Luna heard her heavy breathing and felt the hard grip on her small throbbing arm. The old woman held her with one hand, and with the other managed to open an old thick door to a small dark room. In one fell swoop she heaved the girl in. All the child could do in that instant was to try and hold on with her little fingers to keep the door from closing in on her. But it was too late—the old woman was much stronger than she was. She slammed the door shut and locked it from the outside. All this time the old woman was shouting obscenities and muttering at her.

Luna continued to cry out and weep. She would stop crying and shut her eyes, but then open them up and see the darkness around her and start crying again. She felt like a speck of dust in a mighty wind. The pain from the beating and fighting to get out was exhausting, and her body shuddered from it. She sobbed what seemed like forever.

Suddenly, Luna felt something brush up beside her, and at the same time she heard the most terrible sounds she could imagine. She had heard these noises before and dreaded them. She tried to figure out from where inside this darkness the squeaking came from. Then it happened. Something furry was trying to climb her bare leg. The other furry thing was trying to nibble her toes. She jumped up and shrieked and scratched at the door in panic and desperation. Sobbing and crying out, she stomped bare her feet and screamed. She fumbled around trying to find a way to get away from these hideous creatures she feared. She was in complete darkness.

She squinted, trying to make her eyes see in the dark. Then Luna took a deep breath and regained a sudden calm from inside. She instinctively began to feel the wall directly at the sides of the doorway— something was dangling from a hook. She could barely touch it with her small little hands but, she stretched herself, still fighting off the pests that were now attacking her feet and trying to climb her legs! She scraped the wall but managed to grab the object and pulled it down. In an instant, a loud crashing sound came all around her. Everything came tumbling down. Something bounced and hit her on the head.

Some time had passed, and Luna awoke to a bit of light coming from under the doorway. Her legs seemed pinned down by something heavy, but she managed to pull them out and brought them up close to her body. Her head throbbed, and she felt tired and cold. She felt something furry by her feet. She cringed remembering what had happened. At the same time, the door opened. She heard the slurring of her name. The woman opened the door red-faced, hollering at the top of her lungs, "What have you done, you stupid girl!" She grabbed her off the floor and quickly began to slap her achy head and bottom.

Luna was in pain and started to cry, but she was relieved to get out of that horrible place. The old woman continued her savage attack upon the defenseless young girl and dragged her back to the house by her small limp arm. She pulled her into the kitchen and threw her down on the floor. The girl gasped and winced from the pain inflicted upon her but she did not want to be thrown back into the horrid closet filled with hideous rodents. The woman walked back, shouting slurs and countless other profanities at the child. This beating would not be the last the young girl would receive from the old woman.

Pulling Feet

The Five Freeway whirred by as the frosty midnight air settled in and around the rickety and crumbling windowsills of the old, faded olive green and white two-story apartment building on Daly Street. All that was seen was a ray of light from the streetlamp peeping through the withered edges of the yellowing pull-down blinds. A single blue flame danced upon the dingy ceiling like a jack-in-the-box inside the second-floor right corner apartment.

The flame emanating from the stove top was the only warmth in the room. The six-year-old girl laying in the dark choked the blanket to keep the frigid air at bay—except her feet never seemed to be interested in being under the covers. They just stretched out far away from her body and kept to themselves. She would bend her knees to tuck her legs and feet under her, but when she would go to sleep, they just ended up uncovered.

That night a soft touch awoke her from her sleep. She must not have been in a deep sleep because no one could wake her up once she fell sound asleep. She was lying on her stomach like she always did.

Her legs were stretched out like the number eleven, and both her feet were hanging slightly over the edge of the bed. She felt a set of soft small fingers gently holding onto one of her feet and at the same time yanking her towards the bottom edge of the bed. In that drowsy instance, she froze like a statue.

The hand seemed to caress and pull her left foot. Her mother who was sleeping next to her took a deep breath in and then out, but she seemed so far away because she was facing the opposite direction. The young girl sank her face into her chilly pillow. She began to pray, *Santo angel de mi guarda, Oh Guardian Angel, please save me*. She asked her angel for courage, and she tried to listen for any sound, but all she could hear was the loud beating of her own heart in her ears. She guessed the guardian angel was awake at this time because she immediately felt brave enough to slowly turn on her left side and pull her feet towards her body.

She gradually began to move away, and she felt the slight fingers release her foot. She placed both her feet as close to her body as possible and kept praying and wishing she was just dreaming. Time ticked slowly which made her feel drowsy and she fell back asleep. This time she went off to a deep sleep. The next morning, the young girl awoke. She popped her head from under the blanket.

She was laying on her left side with both uncovered feet dangling off the bed as usual. She cautiously slipped her feet back inside the security of the blanket. The morning light drew an outline of the blinds upon the wall. The blue flame from the stove top swayed in unison from the steady breath of air flowing from the cracks and crevices in the windows. She recalled the events of the night and slowly lowered her head to inspect under the bed. Only a few dust bunnies stood at attention next to her worn fuzzy blue slippers. All was quiet except for the distant hum of the freeway and her mother's gentle snoring. She slowly sat up after inspecting the floor and wondered if her guardian angel had pulled her feet because she wanted to play.

Timber

Jump, jump, on the bed, next stand up straight and close your eyes, say timber in your head. TIMBER. Sandra fell back on the bed; it was a game. The large thump reverberated on the wooden headboard and along the wall of the small house into the bathroom. Her mother sat straight up in the warm sudsy water as she grabbed a towel and shouted out *"¿Que Paso?"* *What happened?* From the adjacent bedroom, a voice hesitantly and numbly responded *"Nada."* *Nothing.* The five-year-old girl did not cry; she was in shock as she grabbed the back of her skull and bounced back onto her pillow. She knew mom would be angry with her. Her small hand tried to massage the bump on her head, but it was sticky, wet and throbbing like a rotten tooth.

Sandra's anxious and drenched mother Laura stepped out of the old clawfoot tub, and hurriedly wrapped herself up in a pink, faded terry cloth bathrobe and toweled her dripping hair. The young girl knelt on the bed as she pressed her hand on the back of her skull, trying to calm the pain. Her mother went into automatic pilot and inspected her daughter's hair searching around for what she knew she would definitely find. A large gash on the back of her scalp was steadily oozing blood and beginning to saturate her brown locks.

In an instant, Laura wrapped her daughter's bloody head in a towel and lectured her about jumping on the bed. Sandra blubbered and began to hyperventilate and then wailed "I'm going to die!" Her mother nervously soothed her. The small round white alarm clock on the dresser said 10:45 p.m. There was no time to wait, or money for the ride to the hospital. The woman's mind raced as she quickly got dressed, grabbed a sweater, her wallet, house keys, and in one fell swoop she grabbed a blanket and enveloped her daughter in it.

Like a short, five-foot Olympian marathon runner, Laura scooped up her three-and-a-half-foot, fifty-pound daughter in her arms and tore out of her tiny home into the coolness of the night. Her little girl clung to her petite mother's neck like a caterpillar on a tree branch. Laura's adrenaline level jumped to overdrive while she sprinted. Her daughter bounced upon her hip and a large stain on the white towel covering Sandra's head began to spread and transform to a rose color.

The neighborhood was still; the slow murmur of traffic and barking dogs was heard in the distance. The girl felt her mother's heart thumping and gasping breath when she stopped at the curb as they crossed the street. By the next block, she was hitting her stride. Her breath was steady, and her daughter began to feel drowsy. Just before the end of the street block, the buzzing of a late model Volkswagen bug sliced through the calm of the evening. The vehicle drove up and then stopped in the middle of the road. A young man with a kind face popped his head out the driver side window and shouted out over the rumbling engine. "You need some help?"

Laura stopped and in a panicked breath looked at the driver, the dark street, and then at her daughter. She shouted back at the driver "My daughter is bleeding…I need to take her to the clinic." The driver offered to drive them to the nearby emergency room about a mile and a half away. She cautiously agreed. The driver got out of the car, opened the passenger door and helped them into the passenger seat. A silver cross swung from rearview mirror as they car engine rumbled down the street. Her daughter was now calm and quiet. The driver made small talk about who knows what.

The car drove past the main drag and then turned left and right again. A neon red emergency sign blinked at the occupants of the Volkswagen vehicle as it entered the driveway of the clinic. Both mother and daughter got out of the car. She thanked and blessed the driver. The car was swallowed up by the night. They shuffled into the clinic as the towel was now a saturated magenta hue. The nurse at the counter swiftly took the little girl down the corridor and placed her on a gurney with the mother in tow.

The nurse removed the blanket and unwrapped the towel on Sandra's head. She pulled out a cart filled with gauze, tape, alcohol swabs, cotton balls, syringes, medical gloves, and bandages. A doctor with a white lab coat, stethoscope, and a toothy grin walked up and began to chatter with the girl and the nurse. They trimmed and shaved away her brown hair around the bloody wound. The doctor handed the little girl a lollipop. She popped it into her mouth.

The nurse gave her a numbing shot, and the doctor began to put in some stitches. Laura stood quietly praying and holding on to her daughter's hand.

The phone rang the next day. One of Sandra's school friends wanted to come by to see her. Everyone at school said hi. They wanted to know what happened. "It was only a game" she said.

May Flowers

White dress, white socks, white shiny dress shoes, a short white veil and a clump of white flowers. Down the aisle I go as everyone watches and prays. There he is looking down at me. He is smiling his gentle smile. His eyes tell me he is not sad. He is happy I am here. That is what I see. I am glad to see him each time I visit.

She is also watching me. She knows that I have been good. I want to bring these flowers to her. She is beautiful. Her face is looking at me with that sweet smile. Her eyes are so warm and kind. Her flowing white dress beneath her light blue robe. A white veil covers her head, and she holds her hands together so gently like butterflies kissing flowers. I wish I could be like her.

We all sit together, and the squeaky bench tells on us. We squirm back and forth in our white crinoline stiff knee-length dresses. All the boys are wearing white button-down shirts and heavily starched pants. Our small feet ache in the shiny white shoes. We sit and listen to the priest. We must not talk or bother anyone. My mother is watching and making sure I am concentrating on the mass. She said I need to pay attention because he is always listening to me and watching what I am doing. I hope so. He makes me feel so special when I see his kind face.

He is also watching me at home. We have a picture of him and statues and crosses. My mother says we have to visit him here in his home because it is the right thing to do. He likes when we visit him. I love the smell of the flowers. They are everywhere in his house.

She lives here as well. She also stays with us, but she lives here too. She is watching over all of us; I like that. Every day in May I am offering flowers like a bride. A boy is sent down the aisle behind me offering his flowers to *La Virgen*. Jesus loves me, and I love Jesus. I have his name. I feel very special.

White dress, white socks, white shiny dress shoes, a short white veil and a clump of white flowers. Down the aisle I go as everyone watches and prays....

Sugar Plum Fairy

"I Saw Her Standing There" by the Beatles trickled out of the doors of the chipped and dilapidated schoolhouse that sat like a wicked old witch with a pointy hat roof and evil eyes for windows, upon the blacktop across from the renovated elementary school building. During the school day, the structure was strictly off limits. Children played dodgeball, basketball, hopscotch, or jumped rope, right outside at the feet of six large steps leading up to the heavy, weathered wooden doors that creaked like an old rocking chair when opened. At the end of the school day, children would stream out of the main school entrance and side gates, towards awaiting buses, cars, and sidewalks. The sagging old building seemed to be holding its breath awaiting the last bell.

Often a cluster of kids hung around a few more minutes to swing from the steel hanging rings or the monkey bars, or flip like a gymnast from a single bar, or punch the tetherball around and around, or glide down a metal slide which all stood at attention by the south side fence. Towards the west side of the schoolyard, a large brown portable building enclosed by a metal fence and gates, shielded by a clump of trees, held the afterschool care. Snacks and an afternoon nap would fill the time in wait of parents who would arrive later for their children. That afternoon the radio DJ introduced Marvin Gaye's "I Heard It Through The Grapevine." Children played along the back fence as the music vibrated against the tattered window sills of the old school. A trio of older children darted around playing tag, while waiting to be picked up. The afternoon sun and squealing of children began to fade, and the music continued to flow through the open door of the old building. The stomping of multiple feet galloped up the worn, wooden squeaky stairs and plodded into the large entryway. "I want to hold your hand" by the Beatles began to blare out of radio speaker.

Mr. Rodriquez a young, lanky, curly, dark-haired supervising teacher stepped into the building. All the kids liked him because he would join games or give homework help. The kids jumped and danced around to the music flooding the entryway. Mr. R, as the kids called him, watched the kids jump around for a while. He went over to an old dusty record player turntable stacked on a short bookshelf in the corner of the room. He lifted the cover and turned a knob. He then placed a finger on a stack of album covers on a table adjacent to the bookshelf and began to flip through the large pile. He pulled out a record and shut down the radio, as the turntable began to spin and the arm dropped onto the edge of the shiny vinyl. The turntable speaker shrieked out as the needle skipped a scratch and then the smooth strumming of a cello, chiming of bells, a bellowing clarinet, and even more bells filled the room and glided out the door. The children in the room paused their dancing and asked Mr. R what song was he playing. He told everyone that it was the "The Dance of the Sugar Plum Fairy," a dance from the ballet *The Nutcracker* by a Russian composer. Some of the children urged him to turn the radio back on. He replied he would–once the song was over. All the kids shuffled out except for one second grader. She stood in the room absorbing like a sponge. The bells twinkled in her ears. The cello and clarinet palpitated in her heart. The musical notes felt like soap bubbles on her skin. The music filled her fingers and toes. She began to dance on her tippy toes. She twirled around and flew into midair.

The music rose and fell, and the girl jumped, leaped, and spun. That afternoon the little Sugar Plum Fairy pirouetted all the way home as her exhausted mother ambled right behind her. That night the young girl babbled on and on about "The Sugar Plum Fairy." Her mother turned on the radio as she always did, and sad Spanish songs began to pour through like syrup through the speaker. The young girl could only hear the bells twinkle and see herself dancing as her mother urged her to eat her dinner. That night she leapt and spun among flowers. The next day the girl could only think about the music and dancing.

During morning recess, lunch, and P.E. she stood atop the blacktop gazing towards the structure stretching her toes wanting to leap in the air. That afternoon the girl dashed into the old schoolhouse looking for Mr. R. Other children ran in and out chasing each other. The shy second grader found Mr. R. helping a few students with their homework at a table in one of the rooms off the entryway. She waited and then timidly asked if he could play more ballet music. His grin filled his face from ear to ear. A few minutes later she stood by the turntable taking in each piece as Mr. R told her about each song and she hung on every note. That evening at home after dinner, songs began to float out like raindrops upon a lake as Bach, Mozart, Tchaikovsky, Beethoven, Shubert, and Brahms played and the young fairy jumped, leaped, spun, and spun, and spun.

The "Yonque", the Junkyard of Things

The Saturday morning crispness struck our faces as we strode down the street. We crossed the intersection and stepped in unison swiftly as the droning traffic of the Five Freeway blew past overhead. Our footsteps and the oncoming street traffic on Main Street echoed and filled the cavernous cement underpass as we made our way to our destination. Mom and I walked upon the cracked and buckling sidewalk pulling our old, rusted, raspy grocery cart. Once we cleared the freeway, we came upon homes which hoarded cats, dogs, or cars and still others who grew junk piles and dry weeds. Some apartment buildings were rickety, and seemed to cling to the foundations from their construction. Others grew from concrete and dressed in a shade of bright yellow, cobalt blue, or avocado green.

We marched silently and purposeful like ants upon a breadcrumb. Our route was set, and the morning chill clung to the air. We trekked like nomads around the neighborhood towards the outskirts of town where empty, dry weed-filled lots and sturdy brick laden warehouses replaced weary apartment buildings and ram shackled homes. We roamed down streets and jay-walked down lonely paths and came to a stop at a busier intersection where trucks chugged, and coughed on their way to the freeway. Mom took my hand and seemed to pick up the pace, and we jogged across the street towards a chain linked fence. Several cars were parked in the distance beyond the fence. If you looked towards the horizon, you could see the L.A. River, Dodger Stadium, the Southern Pacific railroad tracks in the far distance, and still further, the downtown Los Angeles skyline.

However, today we would be arriving at the *yonque*. The *yonque* was a warehouse dock and a parking lot. Every Saturday morning a plethora of items would be piled high all over the lot and dock. A sea of dolls, toys, clothes, shoes, purses, household items, small furniture, lamps, books, and office waste were often found. The parking lot was strewn with these discarded things, and they were up for grabs. People would arrive with a parade of receptacles: bags, carts, baby strollers, store carts, and their cars and trucks to fill and haul away their findings. My mother and I, and other hearty souls, would scour the lot for hours to find our treasures.

That morning we arrived and scanned the scene. Some piles of discards were high and bundled neatly while others were scattered about. Anticipation filled my mother's eyes. She loved to search and find something special. It did not matter that it was rejected by someone else or that it was once someone else's trash. She enjoyed looking for her own buried treasures. Searching through the purses, clothes, shoes, and household items and recycling some old thing. I went directly to the books, toys, and other knick-knacks. Once in a while, you would find pirate treasure. Coins would often fall out of the purses or the clothes. My mother once found a few dollars in a small change purse inside a handbag. She was hooked. I never found any money like my mother had, but I found much more valuable items.

Books...books...and...more...books! I couldn't believe that people threw away books! I would scoop them up quickly and place the ones I wanted in our shopping cart. Often the hardcovers were faded, or the spines were torn. I would find encyclopedias and large dictionaries. Sometimes magazines would be thrown about, and I would pick them up, dust them off and place them all in a stack upon the dock, so people could see them and take them. Other finds I relished were found looking through the office debris. Often there you would find office supplies. Sometimes a pile of pens and pencils would be rolling around in a tray, or clean and crisp typing paper would be bundled with a rubber band and tucked in a clear bag. Those were my treasures. Books to read and paper to write upon were my gems.

Boxes of discarded toys were fun to rummage through, especially dolls. The dolls would be half-dressed. Blond Barbie dolls with missing limbs and mangled hair would be lying next to a one-eyed winking baby doll. At other times if you were fortunate, you could find Barbie's polyester pantsuits and her matching tiny plastic heels. Sometimes Barbie's boyfriend Ken would be with her and that would be a fantastic find. Other dolls weren't as lucky because their eyeballs would be rolling around their heads like a ball in a pinball machine. Many toys had missing or broken parts, and it all reminded me of the Island of Misfit Toys. I would feel sad for disfigured and destroyed toys. I knew those toys would never be saved.

Once the sun began to beat down on our backs, and the traffic would become louder, mom would yell out *"¡Vamanos!"* I would turn around and find her still squatting down and looking at a pair of heels or a pocketbook. She would always be holding different items in her hand and tucked away under her arm, ready to be dropped into the cart. More people would arrive like crows searching for food. Once we were ready to depart my mother would place her treasures in the cart, and I would show her mine. She liked that I chose books and paper items. She would peruse our findings in the cart and smile back at me. We would make our way through the relics and discards of other people and cross the street in unison back towards the neighborhood. We walked quietly and steadily on the sidewalk. We retraced our steps back home as the echo of the freeway grew and pounded our ears. Both in deep thought regaling and luxuriating in the glow of the findings at the *yonque*....

A Lone Tennis Shoe

The day was cloudless, and the air was still, and the hum of traffic was calm on the main drag. A few pedestrians walked down the street doubled fisted with shopping bags from the local Bi-Rite Market on the corner. The local Mexican bakery was buzzing with customers selecting from the variety of *pan dulce* like gold miners panning for gold. The hustle of daily routines filled the day – then at once, the squeal of tires and screams fused in the air. Mounds of people assembled like roaches huddling upon a gob of lard on a stove top as they amassed along the sidewalk. Others spilled out of the local Kentucky Fried Chicken on the corner or stood in disbelief at the gas station. Across the street on both ends, pedestrians seemed like weather vanes pointing this way and that. The chaos was heard up and down the street.

Yells and screams reverberated against buildings and shook the sky like a million screeching guitars. Horror and confusion overflowed upon the faces of the onlookers young and old. Several men ran into the street chasing down a large, white four-door sedan with shiny steel bumpers, as the legs of a young child simultaneously thrashed as they were dragged behind the right-side whitewall tire of the car. Women shrieked in panic as they could not comprehend the horrible situation being played out in front of them. The vehicle had struck and pulled under a tiny body like a shark in a feeding frenzy. The driver had rolled past the two pedestrians calmly crossing the crosswalk; he was oblivious to the commotion occurring just on the other side of his quarter-inch, rolled-up, driver-side window.

The child's mother melted along with her pleas into the pavement as she kneeled, trembled, and sobbed uncontrollably once she realized what had happened. At some point, pedestrians who towed their children held them closer, trying to shield them from the terrible tragedy. A couple of men caught up on the other side of the car and pounded on the trunk and peeled out profanities and shouted, "Stop the car!" at the driver to no avail. A few younger men ran faster as if being chased by a bull on the streets of Pamplona. The men grabbed hold of a door, and still, others tried to jump on the large gleaming hood of the car. Those actions triggered the next events as the driver came to a sudden halt and people roared with pleas for the child's tiny limp body caught between the undercarriage of the car and the gray asphalt.

The blaring of sirens became thunder strikes in the distance as a crowd of people on the pavement began to gather around the driver violently interrogating him. Still, others tried to pull the lifeless child's body from its precarious situation. The child's mother was lifted and held by a stranger trying to soothe her desperation. The child's lone red tennis shoe stood a few yards from where the car came to a complete stop, silently speaking a thousand words. Cars coming from the opposite sides of the street began to turn back onto side streets or cross through the gas station on the corner. The LAPD squad cars, yellow caution tape, and orange traffic cones began to bloom all around the perimeter of the heartbreaking scene. The fire truck, ambulance, and paramedics enveloped the shiny back bumper of the car, lifting and extracting the tiny figure and placing it on a gurney, covering it with a sheet which seemed to swallow the child whole. The police officers began to push pedestrians off the pavement, and some onlookers began to disperse.

The whole event occurred in a brief moment, but the anguish stood around like a stomachache. On the sidewalk, a five-year-old with sad brown eyes had been staring at the lone tennis shoe left behind. The child had watched the flopping of legs behind the tire of the car until the abrupt stop. The gurney disappeared into the ambulance as the hit-and-run driver was gingerly pushed into the police car to separate him from the angry crowd that surrounded him. The sad-eyed child on the pavement was pulled into the present moment by a tap on her shoulder. She began to amble away from the scene staring at the lone bright red tennis shoe with the laces still in a perfect tight bow.

That night the sad brown-eyed child became feverish and had nightmares of flailing legs and squealing tires. She moaned and cried in her chaotic sleep. Her mother that night prayed and cradled her young daughters' restless body until the cries of the nightingale disappeared. Both mother and daughter awoke feeling battered and bruised.

Several days later, the sky was cloudless, the air was still, and the hum of traffic was slow on the main drag. The shadow of a lone red tennis show pierced the memory of a sad brown-eyed child as she walked hand in hand with her mother down the main drag as people walked double fisted with grocery bags from the local Bi-Rite Market as the hustle of the daily routines filled the day.

China Poblana

The thin, silver sewing needle pierced through the stiff, bright red material as the matching thread looped around a small, bright green iridescent sequin. Her worn, delicate fingers pulled the thread carefully trying to leave some space between the many shiny, colorful spangles she had previously sewn on to create a dangling effect. Another hundred vibrant bright flecks laid dribbling out of a small plastic package on the old kitchen table under the dim ceiling light like twinkling stars pouring from the Milky Way.

Margarita had been sitting in the same position adding the decorations meticulously working into the late hours for several weeks, creating a sparkling silver eagle resting on a green cactus holding a brown snake surrounded by colorful butterflies and flowers. The *China Poblana* skirt completed the dancing ensemble along with a white and red trimmed *sombrero*, a white, fringed cotton blouse with colorful embroidered flowers and a large silk band of striped red, white and green material to tie at the waist, and a set of two smaller matching silk ribbons that would create décor for her daughter's braids. A pair of black shiny tap dancing shoes was neatly tucked in their box ready for the *Jarabe Tapatio*.

Her seven-year-old daughter Gabriela was part of a dance group in Boyle Heights. She had been saving whatever extra money she could for months and working extra hours to pay for the dance lessons. The different pieces of the outfit had been expensive. This dream had taken her on many bus trips to various places from the tourist shops at La Placita Olvera on Alameda Avenue, Grand Market on South Broadway in downtown, and El Mercadito on First Street and countless stores in and around Brooklyn Avenue in Boyle Heights looking for a good deal on the different traditional costume pieces.

Margarita wanted a blank canvas of a skirt to freehand her own design. A wizard at sewing and embroidery, she would use her creativity and complete this labor of love. Passing on her culture to her daughter Gabriela was incredibly important. It had always been her duty to give what she could to her child. Making sure her daughter would be proud of the old country, and her Mexican roots were necessary—like breathing.

Margarita's plans for months had gone on so long, and little by little she had gotten closer to her heart's desire. The dance classes were pricey; therefore she could only afford to send her daughter to dance class only once or twice a week. Seeing her daughter's intense concentration and joy in her face as she followed the dance steps and moved to the rhythmical beats of the music made everything worth all the effort.

Each week, the traveling across town on two buses and the long walk to the dance studio created anticipation and excitement for the young girl. The dance group was for six to ten-year-olds. There were mostly girls in the group and sometimes Gabby had to dance the boy dancing parts. She did not mind. She loved every minute of the bouncing, leaping, and stomping steps she was instructed to perform as the *Ranchera* musical beat pounded and reverberated against the walls of the dance studio.

One day the dance teacher announced the troupe was going to give a special performance. The group of girl's oohhed and ahhed, imagining the possibilities. Those able to attend would need the *China Poblana* outfit. The dancing teacher had the group of kids practice the *Jarabe Tapatio* dance steps many times over. Over several weeks the young dancers had performed at a rest home for senior citizens and at an outdoor festival. Watching the children sway, tap, and spin all while smiling dressed in white swirling fringed skirts emblazoned with colorful ribbons made everyone proud. Gabriela enjoyed tapping and swinging her large white cotton skirt to *"La Bamba"* and the Guadalajara dance steps.

Music and dance was always a part of this mother and daughter duo. Music played continuously on the radio and they both often pranced around the house rock and rolling to Little Richard's "Good Golly Miss Molly" or salsa dancing to Santana's "Oye Como Va" in their kitchen. Tear-filled eyes and intensity often blazed in her mother's eyes when she sang old passionate, soulful Yolanda Del Rio and Jose Alfredo Jimenez Mexican songs. Her mother loved to grab her daughter by hand and twirl, Cha-Cha-Cha, or Boogie-woogie dance around the house.

The trips to the dance studio continued, and finally one night the silver needle looped and the red thread was cut as the last sequin and knot was in place. The blouse was pressed gently and lovingly, along with the colorful, shiny skirt that gleamed brightly like a pirate's treasure. The next morning on the 5th of May, the band of girls in full *China Poblana* regalia boarded a white van which made its way onto a busy freeway for what seemed hours. The morning was cool and crisp. The girls, dance teacher, and chaperones stepped out of the van into a predetermined parking lot. The large lot was eerily empty. The sunrise was gently piercing through the eastern portion of the sky, when all at once the girls turned and stared in unison, recognizing their destination.

The amusement park of their dreams appeared before them. The iconic symbols and sites peered out into the morning sky like nuts and marshmallows on rocky road ice cream. The girls giggled and were ecstatic. They all started walking quickly to a gate and then down some corridor and then finally they entered into a shed like building where many other people were running around hurriedly. The dance teacher met someone, and then someone else showed up. They told all the girls to get ready and stay in line. Then they all walked through a door onto an empty imaginative alleyway. Colorful buildings and cobble-stone streets arose as they walked further into the amusement park. Each dancer was positioned up, down, and across the street yards apart from each other. Gabriela was positioned by a red hitching post, formed like a horse head with a golden ring in its mouth. She stood there in awe in the emptiness of the magical main street. She felt anxious about her performance. She had practiced curtsying as she extended her skirt and bent her knees. Her mother had presented the completed version of the skirt that laid almost every day and night on the kitchen table after dinner the night before. The beautiful majestic eagle and snake on the cactus represented many hours of love that her mother dedicated to this endeavor.

Gabby felt itchy, and the tight braids made her head hurt. Someone came on the loudspeaker and then the music started. The dance teacher shouted to start dancing and all at once an avalanche of bodies began to appear, and voices of adults and children strolled in unison, pulling out cameras and adjusting purses and bags. Many of the park visitors were neatly dressed in suits and ties with cameras attached to their shoulders. Still, others spoke in different languages as they carried small children or pushed single or double metal strollers. The music poured and reverberated amongst the cobblestone street and buildings. Couples dressed in summer clothing held hands, stopped and smiled, or just stared and joined the crowd down the middle of the street. Chinese and Japanese visitors stopped to snap pictures at the dancers. The young girl tried to stay in step, tapping her feet in place as she tried to remember all the dance steps to the *Jarabe Tapatio*. The sun began to beat down as the music continued for what seemed forever.

At one point, an Asian couple stopped, smiled and asked Gabriela for a picture in heavy accented English. They smiled at her and pointed to the camera lens. She posed holding her priceless skirt and smiled shyly into the bright sunlight. The amusement park visitors continued to march by the dancers. The music played on as did the dancing. Pictures were taken, and the young girls' faces grew shinier and darker in the sun. Soon the music stopped, and the girls were gathered up. They formed a line and were quickly placed upon a double decker bus which took them around in loop as they waved at the park visitors. Everything seemed to be a blur. The bus ride over, they were hurriedly escorted back through the fancy alley into the shed-like building. Inside they whisked them around countless people rushing in and out dressed in colorful uniforms. The young girl followed her group as she bumped into a headless character and then another; it gave her a shock. She tried to understand what had just happened. How cruel to find out this way? She felt betrayed as a bit of her innocence suddenly slipped away. She felt cheated somehow. Did everyone else know this? Did the other girls in the group notice? How could she not know? The thrill of dancing suddenly became clouded by realizing that things were not what she had imagined them to be.

The group retraced their steps back out into the parking lot to a sea of cars. Somehow the van was located, and everyone swiftly entered and sat quietly looking out the van windows; Gabby relived the whole event and the character encounter was now just an unhappy memory. Hours later they all returned to the dance studios still dressed in their colorful attire. Gabriela and her mother made their way to the bus stop, and on the way they stopped at a local corner market to get a couple of soda cans for the ride home.

A tricolored sequined skirt and two tight braids laced with matching silk ribbons. A red-fringed white *sombrero* and green eyeshadow, pink cheeks, and red lips. Days later, a pair of timid brown eyes and a quiet smile looked far past the camera lens. The picture was taken. The *China Poblana* and *sombrero* were hung up in the closet enclosed in a couple of large plastic bags. One day the lessons were discontinued. The new school year would be coming along with Christmas. Margarita would be saving for new school clothes and Christmas presents now. The music continued to play on the radio. The picture of the young brown-eyed girl with the quiet smile hung in the living room. The dancing also continued....

Don't Speak Spanish

"Don't speak Spanish" the old craggy white-faced teacher snapped, as she peered down her nose and blinked through her black bifocal glasses at the brown-skinned second graders in her classroom. Side looks and hushed whispers evaporated like steam on a bathroom mirror across the room. The weekly spelling list was written on the blackboard in perfect chalk forms. All the children were diligently writing down each of the ten words across their lined-writing paper ten times, trying to copy the flawless print. She glared at each student as she bit the inside of her lip. The severe bun on the top of her blond-haired pointy head pulled an angry expression onto her face. The old woman wore a dull pastel blue dress and matching sweater. She took one of her perfectly sharpened pencils from her desk drawer. She scribbled something on a large white notepad across from her stapler and paper tray on her desk.

All the young brown children were squirming in their seats as they tried to complete the spelling word list. Tapping pencils, loud bursts of nose breathing, nose whistles, and finger dancing bounced around the classroom like ping-pong balls. The old teacher opened her desk drawer and grabbed an old wooden ruler from inside, rose from her squeaky wooden chair and smirked at the children. She began to pace slowly towards the corner of the room, smacking the ruler on her open palm. The sound reverberated against the window panes as the sun streaked across the drop-ceiling and bright fluorescent lights.

The children grew anxious and shifted in their seats and upon their elbows as her square black heeled shoes echoed on the linoleum floor. The teacher looked like a tiger stuck in a cage making several turns in the same place. She began to walk up and down each row stopping and examining each student. The students kept their heads down and pencils on their papers. The teacher's angry expression remained frozen in place as she walked back to her desk. Her light blue eyes showed a quiet satisfaction as she sat down and grabbed some student papers from her paper tray. She began to grade diligently making scratching noises as she added up points.

Most students kept trying to print perfect letters to complete each word on the list. Others peeked at the large black clock hands which seemed to be standing still. Some peered across the room to observe the old teacher. A red-haired boy with freckles and a young brunette at the very back of the room turned and smiled at each other and quietly whispered. They continued to write and talk in a low tone. The boy was telling the girl a silly story, and she grinned, and he giggled at his own joke. At an instance, the room became frozen in time. No one breathed as Old Craggy Face lurched from her chair with the ruler in her hand. The boy turned from the girl and gripped his pencil in his right hand and held his breath.

The teacher quickly stepped up to the boy and took her ruler and smacked his little fist he made as he held his pencil completing the last letter of his third word. The boy winced from the teacher's strike. She stood over him like a vulture about to eat her prey. The boy's eyes filled with tears. He didn't make a sound. All the other students recoiled from the sound of the ruler on the skin. The class felt the pain. They were used to the same treatment from the old craggy white-faced teacher. She was strict and mean. The teacher hated them speaking in Spanish. Every day she scolded them. She warned them that they needed to "Only speak English." The boy wiped his eyes on his sleeve. The teacher satisfied with her action, strode back to her desk chair and resumed her grading. The young girl he was talking to kept her eyes on her paper, but felt anger build up in her throat. The young boy with red eyes and a determined look turned to his friend and resumed telling his story. The girl looked at him half scared and half annoyed. The other students grinned under their breaths as they heard the boy gabbing along in Spanish again. He seemed unfazed by what had occurred earlier. The old teacher's ears and neck got hot, and her temples began to pulse. She told the class to finish their assignment and turn it in as quickly as possible. The students looked up from their work and knew not to complain.

The stubborn freckle-faced boy continued his storytelling. The old teacher with an irritated expression got up from her desk chair and bounded this time with a pencil in hand towards the boy. She stopped in her tracks and stood over him and poked the student's right ear with the eraser end of the pencil. She reprimanded and repeated her warning "Don't speak Spanish" and "I told you to stop talking that gibberish" and "You must speak English." The boy yelled out a frightened yelp. All the students turned and gave her a startled gaze. The girl stared at the teacher, also feeling frightened and mad. The teacher removed the pencil as the scared boy pulled on his ear. The boy began crying louder. The old teacher bellowed at the student to stop his crying.

The students quickly shuffled their papers and whispered under their breaths. The teacher remained calm and walked up to her desk and ordered the students to bring up their completed spelling lists. As the boy continued to rub his ear, he wept quietly while his red cheeks palpitated. He tried to clean his runny nose on his shirt sleeve as the girl spoke to him reassuringly. The morning bell rang, and the class perked up, and the teacher gave the order to line up in rows as she opened the classroom door in relief. The boy and girl walked together outside and began to speak in Spanish....

Stalker

Summer was hot as usual. The sheets stuck to our skin like gum to a shoe. The air was stagnant inside the apartment while the spokes in the fan turned and blew the stale hot air and lint across the room onto the curtains. The old refrigerator hummed its old tune, and the apartment rested its tired bones as the heat of the day dissolved like an ice cube in warm water. My mother breathed slowly as she slept and tried to find comfort in the hot room. I fidgeted with the heat of the pillow that made me only hotter. The night seemed endless on those hot summer nights. Dreams of fresh air filled our brains. Dark shadows peered throughout corners as a single candle-light flame stood motionless, reflecting in the mirror upon the dresser against the far wall. The streetlamp peered through the drawn window blinds and streaked against the drawn curtains in the front room. The light beamed straight through the three-room apartment.

A nightingale sang its midnight song somewhere down the street as the traffic on the Five Freeway hummed its traditional tune. A scratching sound echoed in my mother's ears. She turned her head over, and her hot breath lingered on my face. I pushed my head further into my hot pillow. The next sound pushed against the wall and a deep tone of metal clung in the air. My mother shot up from the bed like steam in a tea kettle. She quietly went to a drawer and wrapped her right hand around the muzzle and placed in her small index finger on the trigger. She quickly slipped on her robe and slippers. She tip-toed and grabbed the broomstick near the kitchen doorway with her left hand. She saw the shadow of the figure in the kitchen window through the thin, pastel yellow, daisy curtains. The gun felt heavy as she tightened her grip. The shadow continued to pull on the window as she pointed up towards the ceiling. She held her breath and pulled on the cap gun, and one short, loud pop was heard. She gasped as she stared at the curtains as the neighbor's backyard light slipped through the fence and exposed the figure balancing upon a small side fence, attempting to climb the metal trash cans against the apartment wall and trying to break into our kitchen by way of the window.

The sound from the cap gun did not phase the figure. My mother yelled out angrily that she would call the police. The shadow of the perpetrator continued its mission; trying to pull up the large kitchen window as he balanced on the metal trash cans. My mother screamed out for help as she pounded on the ceiling with the broom handle and on the wall between the neighbors and us. My eight-year-old stomach and throat seemed stuck like tape. My whole body shook in unison. My mother yelled out to me not to be afraid and to go to the neighbor and call the police. I couldn't move. The individual continued as a blinking light danced across the next-door neighbor's fence. The prowler jumped off the trash cans causing a cacophony of crashing sounds. A yelp was heard and pounding at our front door ensued.

The figure of the suspect was in the police car, and everyone in the apartment house was standing in robes, slipper, and curlers. Other neighbors stood on their porches and stoops watching the show. The police were interviewing my mother and our neighbors. I was still shaking and kept looking at the blinking lights on the squad car. The police officer asked my mother to confirm how many children she had. They asked her about her husband; there was none she replied.

Back inside my mother checked on all doors and windows. She closed the curtains and turned off the lights. It would be a long night. The heat remained, and I felt I would not wake in the morning due to the stubborn heat and airless rooms. The cap gun was placed back in the underwear drawer. The broom was placed next to the back door. My mother brought an old baseball bat out of a large drawer and set it on her nightstand that night. The hot pillow stuck to my sweaty face. I stared up at the ceiling that night listening for every sound and analyzing every dancing shadow from the single candlelight flame which flickered as it melted away.

A couple of days later, two dark-suited detectives arrived at our door. The suspect had confessed that he and my mother had a relationship and that my mother had two children a boy and girl. He also said he had watched us over the course of a week from his car. He had stopped across the street from our home stalking us. My mother turned to me, smiled, and told the detectives that I was her only child. Both detectives looked over at me and nodded their heads in unison like couple of bobblehead characters. Both detectives stepped out into the afternoon sun as both my mom and I stared out the front window, and looked past them across the street from our home.

Double Mint Gum

Early to rise…three city buses from the east side to the west side. Three hours later on a scorching San Fernando Valley summer morning it was eight o'clock on the dot. A scrunched-faced Spaniard woman opened and closed her front door quickly—not wanting to let the cool air conditioning escape. She inspected both individuals that introduced themselves as they entered her sunken condominium living room. The woman's scrunched face unfolded with a scowl and scolding voice. The coldness in her manner felt like the freezer section at the grocery store.

The Mexican cleaning woman and her twelve-year-old Mexican-American daughter scanned their surroundings. The scowling woman gave the ten-cent tour of her home. Her English-peppered voice with a Spaniard accent became a low snarl as she pointed to the guest bathroom. She continued with the kitchen and breakfast nook on the second floor, and the door to her one bedroom suite with master bath. She explained that some loads of wash would need to be done in the basement garage where the washer and dryer lived.

The cleaning lady knew the routine. She had spent her life using her back and hands. Vacuum the carpets upstairs and downstairs. Scrub the toilets. Wash the bed linen in the hot garage. Don't forget to dust and polish everything. Throw out the trash. Mop the kitchen and bathrooms and wash the tubs and showers all in a few hours. The cleaning lady in a sleepy voice instructs her daughter to get the vacuum cleaner out of the hall closet, and the girl begins to vacuum the living room.

The cleaning commences up and down stairs. Sweeping, polishing, scrubbing, mopping, dusting, non-stop. Up and down the garage steps, washing and drying clothes and bed linens. It's noon. Hunger calls out and stabs their intestines like glass shards. They continue to work. They don't stop. The cleaning lady cleans the bathrooms and the girl polishes and vacuums. Her stomach keeps roaring like an Indy car engine. No food to eat. No water. No stopping. Need to finish.

It's 2:00 p.m. All done. Time to leave. The stern-faced woman walks around her condominium inspecting the cleaning results. She carries a check in her hand and two sticks of double-mint gum. She slowly hands the twelve dollar check to the cleaning woman and says, "And here are two pieces of gum for you and your daughter." The cleaning lady replies, "No thank you, we're full." The woman holds on to the sticks of gum. The cleaning lady and her daughter step out into the bright hot afternoon sun after being in the coolness of the air-conditioned home.

Both their stomachs turn somersaults with hunger. The heat makes them feel almost faint. The sticks of gum stick in both their minds. The cleaning woman places the check in her purse and is quiet. Her daughter walks diligently behind and turns to her mother. "What did she mean by offering us gum?" she asks. Her mother replies angrily with tears in her eyes, "We don't need her gum!" Her daughter thoughtfully understood her meaning. She continued "We'll get lunch before we get on the bus." Her daughter began to feel anger rise in her throat.

At that instance, a grinning woman approached them. The woman was another of the cleaning's woman's clients. She was a jovial and gracious Jewish teacher. The Mexican cleaning woman brushed her tears from her eyes and smiled at the kindly lady. The woman hugged them both. The cleaning woman sighed. The woman asked her "What happened? Why so sad?" The teenage girl erupted and told the woman all about the two sticks of gum and their long day. As the girl spoke, the Jewish lady became more and more troubled. She quickly grabbed them by their hands and escorted them back to her condominium. She promptly walked them into her sunken living room and up the stairs to the second floor landing and sat them down in her kitchen breakfast nook. The coolness of the air conditioning kissed their hot cheeks. The lady quickly and diligently mixed some instant iced tea and cold water and filled two large ice-filled tumblers and served them both. She opened her refrigerator and pulled out a large covered bowl. She went into her breadbox and packed four slices with egg salad. The cleaning lady and her daughter were shocked at her kindness. Their stomachs roared in unison at the anticipation of the food to come. The kind woman placed the sandwiches on plates, and she handed them both napkins. She urged them to start eating. She advised the cleaning lady to never return to that client. She continued to talk about how unkind people can be.

Three city buses from the west side to the east side. Three hours later on a scorching Los Angeles summer evening it was 6:00 p.m. on the dot. The cleaning lady and her daughter made it back home with content bellies as they passed their local grocery store with a giant advertisement for Double Mint Gum.

Cardboard Dreams

Like an ancient Aztec ruin, a massive monument surrounded by dirty brown and gray sand stood majestically along a tree-lined pathway at the local neighborhood park on the edge of town. Anticipation filled the crowd of children jockeying for position at the foot of this large triangle. Kids from all around the neighborhood could not wait to scramble up the vast concrete structure with large chunks of cardboard in hand, just wide enough for one or two thrill seekers willing to launch down one of its rough slopping sides.

The golden ticket in the hands of big and small children was found along the way to the park in trash bins or behind an obliging dumpster. Boys and girls would hike up to the top of the pyramid with their paper sleds in hand, ready to propel themselves downward. The process of the journey, mounting, and descending the great monolith would continue all day long and then dissolve in the evening like an ice cube on a hot day.

Many times, the cardboard sleds would tear from the continuous use by the original owner or after a trade with some unsuspecting newbie rider excited to join the crowd. Some kids would rip pants, shorts, scrape thighs or legs. Often sandaled feet would get nicked and bloodied. Cries of happiness and delight like game show contestant winners would be heard all day long. Parents, in turn, would shout out at children to be "Careful!" or "*Dios mio*" and hold their breath as their ecstatic children landed onto the shiny sand granules.

The imposing concrete structure was not the only large mound to scale at the park. Towering eucalyptus trees bordered a large grassy hillside. The gigantic trees stood as spectators to the cardboard dreamers that would sleigh down and overtake the hill. The rise would become overtaken by packs of screaming voices and assaulted by arms and legs sliding down belly-flop style or luge as if in a winter wonderland.

Often on the ride down the slope, gravity would take over and whisk the cardboard from under the riders like deranged magic carpets. Riders would fly one way and floating cardboard would land on the opposite side of the hill. Sliders would roll and land face down in dandelion or crab weed. Laughter by riders and onlookers would be witnessed by those majestic trees standing at quiet attention. A freshly cut hill meant the cardboard sleds could dash down the hill in seconds like a flick of a flame. Dangers did lurk among the grassy slope. A rock would take the thrill seeker like a leaf on a stormy day. Crashing, smashing, and flipping over would be their destiny on that day.

Sometimes the cardboard would get destroyed in a collision with the hill or other riders. Rolling down the hill like a hotdog conveyor would be the next exciting thing to do. There was nothing like rolling around and around down to the foot of the hill. The dizziness in the bright sunlight filled the brain like happiness on Christmas day. The trees swayed in unison as they seemed to enjoy the delight by all the children.

As the jubilation of the afternoon began to wane, the warriors of the hill and the pyramid began to inspect their battle wounds and weave tales of their conquests. Bits and pieces of cardboard lay as remnants which exhibited the triumphs and defeats on that day. As the children walked back home through the neighborhood, they all smiled to themselves and recollected their adventures as they walked past trash cans where they deposited their shredded cardboard dreams.

Summer

Summer was a like a chocolate fudge sundae with the works. In the neighborhood, summer meant late, late evenings roller skating, popping wheelies, running, jumping, laying on thick clumps of grass and sitting on the cold concrete stoop outside our apartment in the shadow of the Five Freeway. Summertime was like a twenty-five cent grab bag at the corner five and dime; it was full of anticipation and promise of things to come. Those last months of school were unbearable while imagining the fun that would be.

Those lazy simmering summer days meant playing Jacks, marbles, and hide-in-seek under a large avocado tree which filled the whole backyard. The trees' great canopy kept us cool and protected from the hot rays of the sun. My friends and I would climb the tree and walk onto the roof of our apartment house and hug the tree's massive branches and follow the ant trails up and down the limbs. During the hot summer days, we rested among its branches and pretended to be in far off places. The tree never bared any fruit. The enormous tree-trunk felt strong and stoic as it stood there, year after year through earthquake or storm. In the evening, the tree became ominously monstrous as its branches transformed into giant arms and crooked fingers in the shadows. The backyard was off limits once the darkness and shadows of the tremendous tree shrouded and transformed the paradise of the day into a spooky evil abyss.

The front stoop at night, unlike the backyard, was our retreat from the dense and hot stagnant air in our apartment. The heat would reside indoors and force us to go outside and stay awake late into the night because the air in the apartment was stagnant and hot. Breathing was difficult and exhausting. Sleeping was impossible and wasteful. Staying up and standing in the cool of the evening made better sense. Lying on hot sweaty sheets that stuck to your body was gross. The exhausted fan would spin dutifully circulating hot musty, dusty air follicles around the room. It would blow the curtains and hum throughout the night to no avail of any comfort. Breathing fiery wisps of air through the night would make your nose dry out which felt like you were slowly suffocating to death.

The hum of televisions and radios set to Spanish stations would bubble up through the air and were often the background noise for late night grown-up conversations and stories of days gone by in the old country. The heat of the night was soothed out on the stoop as cool threads of air swirled around, while we stared up at the sky admiring the glow of the moon staring back at us. The neighborhood was calm and at peace. There would be no traffic on the street, and the brightness of the signal lights would turn red, yellow, and green in the freshness of the evening. The neighborhood seemed soundless, and even the Five Freeway appeared to slow down and only a gentle purr of traffic was heard from the stoop. People that were out late at night would stop and take a breath and expel the heat from their bodies. Late night was a respite from the scorching day.

Summertime was marked by weekly trips to the Downey Park pool for twenty-five cents. The pool packed like a sardine can. Arms and legs flailed about, bodies were breaching like whales and squeaking like dolphins which made for a chaotic scene. On the surface of the pool heat assaulted faces and limbs but underneath the water was cold and refreshing. Bodies cannonballed off the diving boards or shot through the water like a sub missile smashing into other bodies like the fizz in a 7up bottle.

Summers in the neighborhood; anticipation, hot, refreshing, stagnant, fresh, gross, scorching, fizzing, chaotic, smashing, a hot fudge sundae with the works....

Teeth

A woman stepped out of the old downtown brick building still feeling dizzy and holding a wad of tissue to her aching mouth. A child skipped out right behind her. The North Broadway traffic was a blur as they both briskly strode down the street. The pain in the woman's mouth made her wince and pick up the pace as she grabbed her daughter's hand. She could not wait to make it home to adjust the gauze and spit out the out the accumulated blood in her mouth. The iron taste reminded her of the painful journey she embarked on as she watched her upper, and many of her lower teeth disappear at the age of twenty-seven, and the toothless, aged grimace begin to appear in the bathroom mirror. The dentist had "recommended" through his Spanish-speaking dental assistant that all her teeth be removed. She made it sound as simple as removing petals from a daisy.

The constant infections created painful work days and sleepless nights. Baking soda home remedies and over the counter pain treatments had not given her any relief. The choice to see the local dentist and remove teeth had been deliberated over and over as she consulted with her measly savings tucked in her mattress. Her young child peered up through her dark brown bangs with her large chocolate chip pupils at her mother's pain-stricken swollen facial gestures as they waited at the crosswalk. The woman looked down with her red-rimmed hazel brown eyes at her child, and the discomfort radiated like the blinking flames on the prayer candles at church.

The drill continued to make its way around her teeth as water spray, and tooth dust splattered out of her mouth and landed on her fearful juvenile face. The bone-chilling squeal of the drill along with the throbbing in her gums filled her brain, and there seemed no end in sight. This had been the almost weekly routine for several months. Gum cleaning and cavity fillings had been "recommended" to her mother by the local dentist through a Spanish-speaking dental assistant.

Her eleven-year-old teeth began to crowd each other, and a couple of her front teeth decided to step out of line. The BEST SMILE awards she received yearly in elementary school became just a memory of what had been. No money for braces. She was a poor child. Her mother's limited savings would not allow for that luxury. Two years passed and the agonizing trips to the dentist made that now pre-teen feel helpless. Her teeth continued to push against each other like passengers on the afternoon city bus, making for routine cleaning difficult to keep her teeth healthy.

One day, a trip downtown, and then another bus ride further, they arrived at what might be a chance to save her smile. Both mother and daughter walked in towards the entrance to the university dental clinic. They made their way to the front desk where questions were asked and paperwork was completed. They both waited along with others in the lobby and soon her name was called. A third-year dental student introduced himself and began to exam her teeth. He told her to smile and bite down on her back teeth. He pulled on gloves and started to poke around her mouth like she was a pocket full of pennies. The exam only took about three or four minutes. He wore a serious grin.

He then announced, You don't need braces. You would only need them for cosmetic reasons. He asked. You can chew your food, right? He concluded. We cannot help you. We only give free braces to those people who really need them. The questions and comments all bounced around her head as they began their trek back home. The daughter looked at her mother with red-rimmed brown eyes as the disappointment radiated like the blinking flames on the prayer candles at church.

Ants and Ladybugs

Brown ants marched up and down like rugged soldiers preparing for battle upon honeysuckle, twisted yucca squid agave, and the dwarf fountain grass that grew between smooth limestone rock along the dry river bed that bent around the sleepy old town like an old man's crooked finger. The mid-day sunlight beat down on a young auburn-haired girl. Her raggedy yellowy cotton dress clung to her skinny thighs as she squatted barefooted between the stems of grass among the river gravel. The spring rains had come and gone, and the best pools of water were nestled under a top layer of river vegetation. Colorful dragon flies, mayflies, gnats, and other flying pests sped past her ears as the young girl with a stick toppled ant hills and poked under rocks. In the distance, her name echoed, but she did not listen. She was too busy overthrowing ant empires.

Red ladybugs filled tall stems of the green crabgrass growing on a bit of lawn just outside the front steps of the old apartment house on Main Street. The grass had overgrown like a man's grubby beard. The weathered, wooden push mower needed sharpening as it sat on the side of the house behind two aluminum trash cans next to a small white wooden gate. The late afternoon sun glowed on a young brunette-haired girl. Her red stretch shorts clung to her skinny thighs as she squatted barefooted between mounds of green and yellow crabgrass growing among bunches of clover. The summer rains had come and gone, and the grass had grown filling out dirt clumps with useless vegetation. Buzzing bees, dragonflies, and gnats whisked past her ears as she filled a glass jar with the red ladybugs. In the distance, her name was being called, but she did not listen. She was too busy trapping ladybugs.

Rita pulled the aluminum pail from the small water hole emanating from the ground of the riverbed; her small fingers gripped the wooden handle as she had done many times before. A few ants' broke ranks and climbed up her tiny muddy pink toes, and automatically she batted them away. Water splashed out of the pail as she placed it next to the small pool which was surrounded by mounds of fountain grass. With a stick in hand she resumed toppling ant hills. The wind blew through the dry river bend which gave Rita goose pimples up and down her short, skinny legs. In the distance, her name was called, and she was snapped back to the present as she grabbed the handle with both of her tiny hands and quickly trudged, meandering among the river rocks, back up the edge of the river bed pulling the pail behind her.

Ruth tilted the glass jelly jar against the sturdy grass stem and pushed a line of ladybugs into the jar with her index finger. The ladybugs toppled in like red candy apple granules. The bugs struggled up the glass one on top of another; wings opened and then closed, and exhaustion overtook the tiny scarlet beetles. Some managed to escape the glass jail and landed on Ruth's long deep brown locks of hair. Soon they gathered renewed strength and flew over to another grass stem further away. The hum of the Five Freeway and the buzz of street traffic was a symphony that accompanied her ladybug imprisonment. She placed the cover back onto the jar and inspected the ladybugs as they climbed up and slid down the sides of the glass. Some ladybugs were red and spotted, others had an orange hue with perfectly black circles. Their wings were translucent and delicate like tissue paper. A banging at the front window and the call of her name jolted her back to the present as she held on to her ladybug jar and skipped up the stairs.

Rita, the young auburn-haired girl, skipped back to her adobe home with the pail in tow, spilling water here and there and all over her cotton dress. Her sunburnt face held a set of sad light brown eyes and dark brows that gave her an inquisitive look. She stepped into the earthen floor with her tiny, dirty feet and wet dress as she was scolded by an older sister. Her mother was standing over a wooden bowl of raw corn masa and diligently pressing the balls of dough with the palms of her hands to make a perfect round circle and then quickly toss it onto a cast iron comal to heat the corn tortillas. She was working on one of the several dozen batches since early dawn. The water was needed to mix some more dough to continue the process, and Rita was needed to help with the grinding stone. There were several bags of corn kernels belonging to townswomen who could pay a few cents for someone else to make the daily batch of tortillas for their regular meals. The job was painstaking every day—grinding corn, mixing of dough, and pressing tortillas between tired palms for a few centavos to feed the family of five. Rita arrived late, dirty, and wet. Her mother sighed and asked she be cleaned up. Her older sisters scolded the youngest of the bunch and pulled her out of her wet dress and underclothes. She was scrubbed with an old rag and rinsed with the cold water from the pail. Her yellowy dress and underclothes were replaced with a replica—a bit more tattered but clean just the same.

Ruth the brunette-haired girl walked into her apartment with her bug jar in hand and dirty feet. Her sunburnt face held a set of sad, dark brown eyes and dark brows that gave her an inquisitive look. Her mother scolded her for not wearing sandals and catching ladybugs. It was dinner time. Her mother had been counting pennies and placing soda glass bottles she collected in a large paper bag. She needed to make ends meet; she would sell the bottles to the corner market for a couple of dollars. Money was tight. Her mother sighed when she saw Ruth's dirty feet on her clean kitchen floor. Her mother grabbed her and pulled her into the shower. When she reappeared, her long wet hair was wrapped in a towel and she wore faded purple PJs with tiny daisies and her shiny toes glistened in a pair of gray open-toed slippers as she and her mother sat in front of leftover day number three. Warm tortillas covered in a kitchen towel waited to be sprung and filled before the steamy warmth escaped.

Rita in her yellowy dress watched the barrel end of the treinta treinta rifle aimed at her head as she stubbornly refused to sing. Her desperate mother stood between her tiny daughter and implored her drunken husband not to shoot. The little auburn-haired girl looked straight at her father's glistening droopy eyes. He continued to point the barrel demanding that the pajarito sing. This was not the first time her father demanded at the point of a barrel. This was not the first time she had refused. Rita kept silent as her mother gasped in between sobs and prayers. Eventually, the rifle became too heavy in the hands of the drunk. Her mother quickly took the rifle from the hanging strap as his eyes became two slits. Rita would escape back to the riverbank to topple ants.

Ruth in her blue blouse and blue stretch shorts stood in the corner of the room as the large dark, menacing form stood there with clenched fists and enraged nostrils before her. Her mother had been locked in the kitchen with a warning of death. He had slammed her into the kitchen and pushed his young girl into another room. He demanded she call him 'father.' The brunette-haired girl stood stubbornly quiet staring up at this hulking man not responding to his demands. This was not the first time he had demanded at the point of a fist. Ruth kept silent as her mother pounded on the door sobbing that he not hurt her child. Eventually, the beast succumbed and turned back to the kitchen door and walked in and punched her mother in the jaw and walked out. Both Ruth and the ladybugs escaped out the front door.

Mexican Only Child

You're the first the middle and the last
Nowhere to go when life storms arise
You're the oldest and the baby at the same time
Decide, don't whine
A latchkey kid with the key around your neck
Only for your eyes
Do not let others know where you go little one
You need to hurry down the street and keep your head
down
Only child
do not make eye contact with strangers
No brother, no sister to hold your hand
You must be special! You must get everything?
People say
Not special just alone when you're afraid, no one
notices
When you cry no shoulder, no umbrella for the
raindrops
Only child
Beware of those near you too
They say they care?
You see rats everywhere on two legs
they might just nibble your toes
they make you look the other way, be careful
Only child
Independent and self-sufficient, an island onto your
self
Keep quiet. Don't speak. Don't be noticed
Protect your shores and stay afloat

When the tsunami hits or volcano erupts
Only child hold on tight, don't drown or get burned

You are an only child? People scolded you can't be
Mexican
You need to be a member of a bunch like tamales in
la olla
There are numerous mouths, not just one
What family! They jest. You are not Mexican!
If you were, you would have brothers and sisters too
many to take care of
Mexican only child you're as mysterious as the
legend of La Llorona
You have no one to fight with or share things with,
how does that go?
You do not know about hand me downs and sharing
mama and a papa
What do you know about being in a real Mexican
family?
What is a Mexican only child? Is that like la Leyenda
de la La Bella Durmiente
A real Mexican family flows like a waterfall into a
raging river
An only child family flows gently as a bubbling
brook

Mexican Only Child
Grow up fast and help your parent
Don't close your eyes everything is coming your way
No, where to run or hide
You see the lies, hate, prejudice, and sadness
Are you scared little one? No one to comfort you?

Do you need to tell? No time for despair too much to do

Be strong, be wise, observe and learn

Mexican only child is what you are

You are special and unique and a survivor

Don't worry about what the people say

Mexican only child, you are strong as an Aztec warrior and resilient as the land of your ancestors

Candy Striper

As she entered Ward 2025 on Wednesday afternoon, the pungent smell of hospital disinfectant permeated and bit her nose. She held a heavy black tray with five large sterile Styrofoam drinking cups filled with rattling ice chips, water, and a flexible white straw. A voice growled out "Hey, can you buy me a candy bar?" The request came from a young guy with a pleading face with a large mustache, a small goatee and too many tattoos to count. He was trying to reposition himself, his blood-stained hospital gown, and his folded bed sheet on his creaking metal hospital bed. As he moved a sloshing sound came from a large plastic bag attached to where a portion of his stomach used to be.

The human fluid swirled and swished around like detergent inside a washing machine as he tried to gain some comfort from his painful position. He waved his hand with a half-crumpled up dollar bill and flailed his arm to get her attention as she moved methodically towards his side table. His other hand and arm were in a cast, and one of his legs was hanging in a sling suspended from a metal pole like a fish on the line. She placed the black tray with a thud upon the side table next to the bed while desperately trying to not stare at his churning stomach fluids and answered his supplication with a "Sorry can't buy any snacks or food for patients."

All candy stripers were under strict orders not to buy or bring anything to the patients other than water, pillows, blankets, or tissues. He dropped his arm down in frustration, and his plastic bag splashed as he grumbled painfully under his breath. She apologized again, but that did not stop him from repeating his request. She felt uncomfortable denying him but she continued her work and replaced his water cup and walked out of the ward. Throughout the late afternoon and into the early evening hours she went in and out of wards hearing pleas of hunger or agony.

The school counselor told Sonia she needed to catch up on her school credits to graduate. The words on the flyer indicated: "Complete 100 hours and get high school credits as a candy striper." Earlier in the year, she had messed up, ditching classes and hanging out with her "homies." She had to step up and get her shit together or else life at home would be impossible. She told her mother that she would be earning credits for school which was true, but she did not tell her the real reason why. The following week during a trip to the local Zody's department store she bought a crisp white nurse's uniform and a pair of comfortable white Oxford walking shoes to match. The head nurse had given her a red and white candy-cane-striped apron to wear over her outfit which completed the uniform. It made her look professional. Her schedule was to go in a few times a week for 4 hours.

At the check-in office on the first floor of the hospital, Sonia would sign in and her ward assignment was waiting for her. Up a few floors in the elevator, a stern and thorough registered nurse taught her how to wash down and disinfect a bed, and make perfect hospital corners with the sheets. The nurse gave her the tour of the storage rooms where a bunch of supplies lay anxiously waiting to be used. The nurse had her stacking black trays on the counters, and filling large water pitchers to place in huge refrigerators. She was ordered not under any circumstances to buy food or otherwise provide food to any patient; it was strictly forbidden. They told her to stick to her duties and stay away from the patients.

As the days went on her routine was set, and Sonia completed her tasks as given. She got used to the disinfectant smell, bloody hospital gowns, bodily fluid-stained bed sheets, and throw-up tubs. Entering and exiting wards like a phantom and leaving behind water pitchers and cups filled with ice and a bendy straw was her daily function. One afternoon she walked into Ward 2022 where a small skeletal hand dangled from underneath a white sheet. A whimpering, insistent voice cried out in despair. "Please, I'm hungry" it said. She had heard these piteous voices regularly as she made her rounds, but this voice just seemed so much more wretched. As she came closer towards the hospital bed, two sunken eyes and a small balding head with wisps of cotton-white hair emerged from underneath the crumpled sheet. The emaciated individual with a gaunt face stared back at her. "Please, can I have something to eat?" the voice sputtered out a reply. The standard response gurgled up in her mouth and pressed on her lips. She couldn't repeat it to this person. "I'll see what I can do?" Sonia muttered as took a long breath which only made her feel worse as she thoughtfully stepped away from the room into the corridor.

Her rubber sole shoes made a squishy echo along the marble corridor as she walked towards the door that led to a storage room. The storage room she walked into had a sink, two refrigerators, shelves, counters, and cabinets filled with blankets, towels, plastic, and cardboard boxes filled with different medical supplies. She knew that the large refrigerators were filled with plenty of chocolate, rice, and gelatin puddings, small red apples, orange juice cups, and other leftover goodies from uneaten or mistaken diet trays. She also knew that in the cabinets, cookies and other snacks were housed. Surely, she could try to sneak some of these over to that patient to stop the agony of hunger. Sonia looked towards the door and then stared into the refrigerator.

All at once the door to the storage room opened, and a stern-faced nurse strode in. Sonia caught her breath and closed the refrigerator door slowly. She felt the nurse reading her mind. The nurse grumbled and said, "Looking for a snack?" She turned and nodded a quick no. The nurse continued "They need help in Ward 2019." She hesitated and all at once in one fell swoop her words spilled out like an erupting volcano and said to the nurse, "The patient in Ward

2022 is starving." The nurse turned and irritated said, "Yes, I know." The nurse did not blink, and her mouth and brow gave a menacing expression. At this point, she knew that no matter what argument she tried to make it would not move this nurse. Her hands were tied. With that, the nurse turned and went about her business of getting supplies from one of the shelves.

Her heart felt heavy as she walked down the corridor and past the withered patient. Sonia ambled into Ward 2019. A steely nurse stopped at the doorway and told her ten beds needed to be wiped down and made-up. Before she knew it, the end of her shift had come. She decided to go to a special place where she knew it was a different world. She knew of this location because she had peeked in once before. She rode the elevator all the way to the top floor of the hospital feeling excited and anxious. She stepped out and heard the whimpering, gurgling, wailing, bawling, and weeping. However, these sounds did not bother her as much as when she heard it in other wards. She walked down the corridor and saw other people standing before a large glass window.

There on the other side of the glass flailing hands and arms moved in unison. Mouths and eyes opened and closed, and red faces and cheeks colored the scene. The crying continued, and nurses covered heads and wrapped bodies in blankets. There the crying patients were cuddled, fed, and embraced. All the patients were asking for food or comfort, and no one was ignored. The newborn ward was her favorite because kindness abounded there. She looked through the glass and watched as the babies were taken care of and she wanted to jump in and help. She stared for a while and then turned and walked back to the elevator. She contemplated on the patient clinging to life, or so it seemed, in that ward. She thought that patient once was a baby just like these in this ward. She had been cuddled and fed but now ignored and rejected.

The last day came, and a little ceremony took place. A blue certificate was handed to her with 115 hours stamped in with her name. Sonia turned in her candy-cane apron and stepped out into the warm late afternoon air. She walked down the massive cement front steps of the hospital and looked up to the top where she had been working for those couple of months. She would get her school credit to graduate. She would not disappoint her mother. She had accomplished many different things. She became a bit more patient and aware. She learned one significant thing though...she would never want to work in a hospital again.

Drive By

An old yellow school bus chugged and moaned to a curbside stop through a cloud of engine fumes. The squeaky bus door swung open and spewed out bodies that instantly coagulated as one large mass on the sidewalk and then dawdled together in and around the corner liquor store. In a split second a loud popping sound like a firecracker reverberated against the wall of the liquor store. A dark compact car swerved as it sped down the street and then suddenly slammed on the brakes as it came upon the intersection. A group of heads swayed in unison like bowling pins in the car. Everyone on the sidewalk and by the liquor store wall quickly reacted to the bang and ducked, turning their attention towards the revving car. Across the street, bodies poured out of the school entrance and raced towards the intersection to gawk at the scene. Everyone craned their necks to identify the suspicious car.

The crowd of students standing by the wall threw out hand gestures and some profanity, but the culprits in the compact vehicle did not stay around to confront the onlookers' attacks. The entire moment seemed to be in slow motion but at once there was a screech and peel out. The car turned the corner and zoomed, disappearing up the hill. Across the street, the blaring school bell ordered the school narcs to run out and prompt the crowd to get to class. A black and white had shown up just as the compact car sped away in a dissipating cloud of muffler exhaust. The principal and the other school administrators pulled out the bullhorn and began to round up the students escorting them back to the school entrance. The cops pulled away with all lights and sirens and sped towards the direction of the suspect car. The group of startled and confused students across the street rose and straightened up from their squatted positions. They strode apprehensively to the corner and stood to wait for the signal light to turn to go on their way.

Everyone waiting for the light seemed to be breathing deeper and were somewhat pensive, when suddenly a bright, reddish blotch glowed and caught the eye of a girl standing directly behind a boy with a bright, white t-shirt. The small spot seemed to be slowly saturating the boy's right shoulder sleeve. The boy was oblivious to the situation that was occurring. She elbowed her friend who was next to her and pointed at the crimson spot on the shirt. The girl's friend gave out a shriek, and everyone turned towards her. The girls pointed at the boy's shoulder and said: "He's bleeding!" Those around them turned towards the girls and the boy and pointed to his bloody shoulder. He had turned around and saw the startled faces of the crowd staring at him. He looked down his right shoulder and saw the bright red stain and pulled up on his sleeve to take a closer look and found an almost perfectly round hole that had torn through his crisp starched white t-shirt.

He pulled up his sleeve to further investigate this foreign object that had pierced his body as everyone stopped and encircled him. He became frustrated with the situation and quickly pulled and tugged off his shirt. His A-shirt underneath gleamed a milky white and had not been touched by the wound. The girls handed over a handful of tissues they had collected from their friends to him, and he roughly cleaned away the blood on his shoulder. There was a small bullet entry hole that had sliced through his smooth, tough brown skin. There was no exit bullet wound that anyone could see. Everyone asked how he felt as he nervously smiled and neatly folded his t-shirt and placed it on his left arm and said he did not feel a thing. The street light suddenly changed, and bodies began to flood the intersection. The wave of people crossed the street towards the school entrance. The wounded boy turned and started walking towards the crosswalk. His friends walked alongside him and crossed the street. The principal was standing on the sidewalk prodding the students to get to class as everyone crossed the street. The girls exclaimed anxiously the boy had been shot and everyone in earshot gasped. The principal quickly gathered up the boy and radioed the office clerk to call the paramedics. The boy was swept into the school along with all the other students.

After school, a yellow school bus chugged and moaned to a curbside stop through a cloud of engine fumes. The bus door swung open and gobbled up bodies....

Pep Squad

Flying eggs hit the windows and dripped in a globular jumble as shouts and curse words assaulted ears and tempers. The yellow and black school bus snorted and flatulated gas fumes as it revved and held in place, while a handful of pom-pom, saddle-shoed girls bounded up the steps as their orange accordion skirts swung and rested on black plastic squeaky seats. Squeals and profanity babbled and exploded out of the gaggle of girls wearing pep squad emblems emblazoned upon their burgeoning bosoms. They cackled at the pack encircling the bus. Some of the girls made finger gestures and yelled out obscenities through the egg slicked windows. The bus driver turned and shouted back to the troupe to sit down and stop the screaming. The bus engine roared as the rest of the squad scampered on and sat down to hide from the angry attackers.

The rowdy pep squad had struck again. The girls had been banned from other high school football games and practices because they were too loud and boisterous. The pep coach had had difficulty recruiting squad members. School spirit was limited to the popular crowd types. So when a handful of uncharacteristic girls which typically did not participate in the school's extracurricular activities decided to sign up and show some school spirit, the coach was excited to have them join her squad. The pep squad's enthusiasm became a problem during afternoon practice for the football team. The team often had difficulty calling plays due to the echo of the loud cheering coming from the animated pep members. Both squads - cheer and pep - often shared practice time which became a contest of wills. Both tried to out shout and out spirit each other. The cheerleaders were no match for the wildness of pep group. The cheerleaders would smirk, and eye-roll at the squad but the pep rowdies would just mad dog them back. During the football games, the girls yelled and screamed their hearts out so loudly that the roar from the small crowds that attended the games could not match them. Everyone gawked and was annoyed by them, but they enjoyed the attention. Being rowdy was part of the plan. They had earned their tough girl reps in the neighborhood. Now they had a captive audience to indulge their egos. They would not disappoint.

The bus rolled away with the raucous squad squealing and shrieking out the school bus windows; the pep coach scolded to no avail. The school bus careened down the freeway and crossed the city back to the neighborhood. The bus came to a rolling stop across from their home school. The exasperated bus driver released the doors and immediately expelled the contents from the bus and swiftly shut the doors and roared away in a cloud of engine vapors. The pep coach rolled her eyes and stomped away as the girls swarmed onto the sidewalk like a flock of flamingos as they preened and patted their accordion skirts and giggled, recounting the events to each other. The girls had been warned, scolded, and told not to take part in such a display of school spirit by their homies; those street "soldiers." This school participation was against their street code. Their cred would be questioned as true homegirls. Being part of the school establishment was not something you wanted to be part of.

The girls strutted and crossed the street as their orange skirts swished in unison and pom poms bumped back and forth upon their black and white saddle shoes. They enjoyed the ogling stares from the crowd of "tough" boys on the corner. They loved ignoring their whistles and jeering remarks. The girls knew all those boys. They were the homies. The boys swarmed at the flock of girls like gnats over a dewy grassy field. They began to jeer, taunt, and belittle the girls. The pep squad homegirls just laughed and giggled at the boys. They turned and walked away mischievously shaking their hips as their accordion skirts shimmied and pom-poms bounced down the street.

La Vida

She stood in front of the coffin in the small church wondering what had happened in such a short time. She stared at the perfectly placed large funeral wreaths behind the white coffin. She was confused. How could he be dead? This little boy, barely fourteen years of age, a child in her eyes, not an old person's corpse which had lived a whole lifetime of happiness and sadness.

No! A child! Who not so long ago was dealing with pimples and girls. What transpired to create this horrid scene? Someone touched her arm to keep her moving past the bright white coffin. Teresa could not seem to move fast enough for the crowd. Everything to her appeared to be moving in slow motion. She suddenly lost all sense of self and floated above this sight of death and sadness. A figure grabbed her arm and spoke quietly to her in some weird cosmic fuzziness and then she was back on her feet, standing at the end of the coffin, staring somewhere unknown.

Someone tugged at her coat and she turned around. It was her best friend with black tears running down her face. Teresa stared at her friend and looked back at him lying there so young, and so perfect; his sweet face covered with all that make-up and while wearing his Sunday suit was too much to accept. She robotically made the sign of the cross and ambled back to the pew to where they both were sitting. She looked up at the enormous cross where Jesus was looking down at her in his suffering pose. She said a short prayer for his young soul and hoped that he would be with God soon.

Teresa watched how bodies moved towards the coffin and kneeled or just stood and cried over his body. Others prayed and kissed his check or touched his cold fingers. She thought *he must be freezing although he is wearing a nice suit probably the first suit he ever owned in his life.* Oh! *But he was dead, he had no life.* Still, others seemed not to be looking at him in the coffin as they walked past. They seemed almost afraid to look at their future. They knew that the life they lived would only end in this same position "face up in the box." She knew that they were right—no one could get away from that ending if they kept living that CRAZY LIFE.

Why would they choose to live like that? She wondered GOD did they not realize the pain and agony they were putting their families through? What was going on with these people? JESUS, *make them understand.* ONE OF YOUR OWN IS LYING IN BOX, AND HE IS ONLY A BABY!!! Teresa looked intensely at the figure of Jesus, trying almost to force him to come to life so that he would knock some sense into these people, but of course, it could not happen because GOD had tried to change them, but they would not listen. Her friend whispered and pointed to his family which was going up to the coffin crying and holding on to each other. They grabbed on to the coffin sobbing, weeping and making gurgling noises. She wanted to stand up and scream out, WHY WERE YOU NOT THERE WHEN HE NEEDED YOU!

Teresa had known him as part of the crowd hanging out in the school quad. This young kid would hang out with the older guys, the sixteen and older pack. He wanted to be just like them, all tough and scary, but smooth and cool with the girls. He tried to fit right in and be just like them. He tried, but he was too sweet and young to pull that off. He mostly hung with the girls trying his smooth moves, but everyone just laughed them off and thought he was cute. He was everyone's little brother. That's what she called him. She looked out for him and gave him advice. She told him to do good in school and stay away from the trouble that circled his life, day in day out. She wanted him to conquer "*la Vida*" the "Life," but it was impossible now that he was DEAD in the box, in the wooden coffin, and now he would be placed in the cold and dank earth forever and ever. GOD this was too much. She needed to get out of that place. Teresa grabbed her friend's arm, stood up and looked around at the crowd in the church. It was full. She wanted to know where had all those people been when he had needed them. Where were they when he was killed by those guys, who came into to slaughter a lamb? Where were they when these people ran over his little thin body over and over again to make sure he was dead? Where were they to help the family rid themselves of the drug infested life they led? Where were they to help support his future? Where were they? She looked around, and they were all there, just staring almost guiltily trying not to be seen....

Nutrition

Trash cans crashing all around, chaos ensues, and hell breaks loose. Boys were running towards each other like gladiators engaging in mortal combat. The nutrition bell had rung, and it was round one of a daily event at school. Boys who had strutted like peacocks in their street threads through the hallways and into the classroom became enraged and somewhat possessed at the ceremonial striking of the bell. There would be boys who clutched other boys by the neck like *Lucha Libre* wrestlers, or Muhammad Ali enthusiasts who shuffled feet and swung hard rights and lefts at their opponents. Some girls would stare in disbelief or assist the participant by holding coats or books.

School officials would run around trying to disengage bodies and dissuade crowds to move on to snack lines. All at once, the free-for-all would dissolve into physical exasperation by the contenders and frustration by the administrators and campus school narcs. Nutrition time would continue into the next bell, and then single scuffles at opposing sides of the campus would arise again, and the teacher on duty or other school administrators would half-heartedly break up the ruckus. Some students would begin to crowd around, but it would be quickly dissuaded by the emphatic yelling and screaming of admin for everyone to "Get to class!"

Often the nutrition fiasco would leak into lunch and maybe, just maybe, it would last until after school. There would be a showdown on the way home, on some street or at the park. There, the two gladiators would strut and name-call and demand respect by pummeling the other one in the face. The next day at school there would be empty chairs of those individuals carried away in battle to lick their wounds at home. The winner would strut and shake his feathers around, extolling his magnificent boxing attributes.

Sometimes, and this was rare, girls would take part in these events and boys would hoot and holler for blouses to be torn or ripped apart. They would envelop the females in a circle and roar in praise of the spectacle. Girl fights were not about strength, power, or might. Girls would often fight over boys, dirty looks, and beauty. Boys enjoyed the homage that girls paid them, so watching them fight was definitely a spectator sport. Yes, nutrition was a snack and a show…ding…ding...take your places and come out swinging.

Graffiti

Pssssssssst......the sound of the spray reverberated in the cavernous restroom. The acrid black paint aroma perforated the dank, stench of urine among the group of onlookers. Four unusually silent heads swayed back and forth as if watching an intense tennis match. Pssssst......continued the spray, overhead and across the wall as bold black calligraphy coated white egg-shell paint. "It looks good," said one of the girls. The others echoed her approval. The aluminum trash can danced beneath the feet of the tagger as she balanced herself precariously atop the lid. Everyone oooohed and ahhhhed in whispers at the magnificence of their nicknames in print. The girls' giggles rang out like Christmas bells and ricocheted among the restroom stalls. The lookout shushed the girls and flailed her hand and arm to quiet the assembled.

The names Dreamer, La La, Caspar, Chela, and Shorty all glistened like black diamonds across the wall. Dreamer, the artist, triumphantly smiled as she jumped off the trash can gripping the spray can when she finished the letter "Y" in Shorty. She smiled like she had received an "A" on a spelling test. Everyone felt joyous at the outcome. They whispered to each other breathlessly about their achievement. The wall had been defiled and left as a testimonial for all to see. The girls stood around admiring the wall. Chela felt a twinge in her belly. She was uncomfortable with the outcome. She never had her name written on a wall before. She never had the urge to vandalize anything other than her Pee Chee folders. She understood the consequences if they were found out. The school narcs and gang police would be notified, and shit would definitely "hit the fan." Her mom would find out about everything, and that would be the most horrific thing in the world.

She looked up at the glistening letters and knew there was no turning back now, and she walked out of the restroom. She stepped out into the mid-morning dew. The air was crisp, and everyone huddled around deciding their next move. Ditching class and putting graffiti on the restroom wall, all in one early morning, was exciting. The park was quiet except for the chirping birds and cawing crows arguing over territory. The girls strolled through the park; the graffiti would be just a memory now. They would never see it again because that restroom was too far from their usual hangout at the park. The names would only be whitewashed the next day by a park custodian, who would curse those girls to high heaven, while slathering white primer over the shiny black glossy letters....

April Birthdays

They said her half-naked body was found dumped up on the hill at the park. The rumor was that she was victim of an obscene attack by a pack of guys. Others preached she was asking for it when she accepted to go out with some guy. Still, others believed guys from another neighborhood had committed the act. Everyone said…and...then…just like that, they stopped saying…as if nothing had happened. Sometime later at the funeral, many people assumed that her face was so bruised and disfigured it would be difficult to look at. That must be why the family had requested a closed casket. Many commented that the family wept and moaned over the coffin. Much later, everyone insinuated the family knew who it had been...who had done it all. It had been revenge, some kind of payback. They insisted that the family had known the truth. They knew who and they knew why...

No one mourned that Letty was only fifteen and her birthday was only two days away. No one would ever know how she had planned to spend her April birthday at the park, at her favorite hang-out spot by the fence next to the pool with her friends. No one mentioned her plans to splurge and buy chips, soda, candy, and one of those big pickles in the big jar at the corner market across from the park that made her make a funny grimace when she crunched down on the tart, sour, crunchy flesh. No one noted how she just wanted to hold hands with a cute boy she met in her English class at school. There were no rumors of her dreams of getting an afterschool job.

No one revealed how sweet, trusting, and insecure Letty felt when the boys at school called her name and whistled at her. No one recounted how she laughed at her friends' stupid jokes, danced, and sang to the oldies playing on the boom box. No one remarked how much she loved hanging out with her older friends at school who talked about things she couldn't ask anyone else. No one knew that she and one of her friends had the same April birthday. Her friend would turn eighteen and her, an innocent "Sweet Sixteen" on the same day. No one would point out that another baby would replace her after her death. She would be a breeze in the wind…the last period on a page.

No one would remember Letty once walked across a field of dewy grass on a hill as dusk settled over the city and his hand squeezed her gentle fingers through his. No one would ever know that her heart fluttered about like a giant wasp flinging to its death against a streetlamp, as he wrapped his arm around her shoulders. No one would discern that she was unaware of what could happen up on the hill. No one would appreciate she agreed to go out with him because she was flattered and he was a friendly acquaintance. No one would realize that as darkness closed in she would feel unsure of the next moments.

No one would recognize that the drink he offered and her uneasiness to be impolite would carry her away to a darkness that was waiting below for the signal. No one could imagine a nightingale whistle, and a scuffling of footsteps in the darkness would be her conclusion. No one would hear the muffling cries and whimpers permeating from the gentle angel being crushed. No one would cry out and stop those dark figures from enveloping her and discarding her like a piece of crumpled-up paper.

In April no one is aware that someone remembers those oldies playing on the boom box. Someone remembers a sweet girl laughing, singing, dancing, and eating those pickles from the big jar in the market across the street from the park....

The Boulevard

Zzzzzzzp......swoosh......zzzzzp......swoosh.
The sound of the hydraulics humming along as
cherried-out lowrider bombs inch down the street.
Raspy speakers blaring Santana, El Chicano, Kool
and The Gang, and War flood the air. Hoots and
hollers, and nightingale whistles on a crowded
boulevard night. Everyone is out and about. The
KRLA oldies station blares out musical requests, and
the cassette and eight-track players are in overdrive
overdosing on Mary Wells or The Gap Band. Cars
drop down in unison and scrape the pavement and
sparks fly like Fourth of July sparklers. The music
sways passengers and drivers, reverberating across
the storefronts like a waterfall. *Vatos* and their *rucas*
strolling on the sidewalk stop and watch the
cavalcade of *firme ranflas* making their procession
down the main drag like colorful parade floats.

Hand gestures are thrown into the air like confetti
as laughs and giggles ping-pong from street to car.
Mustached or clean-shaven faced drivers wearing
starched and pressed blue or red bandanas and dark
sunglasses are cooed and kissed by a snuggling *hyna*.

Black Fedora hats perch upon pompadoured *vatas locas* checking their heavy-laden make-up and double eyelashes in parked car side mirrors on the boulevard. The music rises and falls as the low rider cars pull in and out of the avenue onto side streets and burger stands to meet up with homies.

Tonight on the boulevard a *firme* movie is playing at the local theatre. The *vatos* and *rucas* begin to arrive and eyeball each other. Couples enter the movie theater hand-in-hand or in groups. The movie theatre fills up quickly, and jeering and whistles from the crowd begin to mount as the movie begins. A low murmur rises and falls as gangster scenes flicker across the movie screen from the assembled crowd. Once the movie ends *vatos* rise and stand in their peacock stance as they smooth their hair, Pendleton shirts, and their Khakis' precisely folded pleats.

Their *rucas* check their cherry lips, cheeks, and pompadour hair. Single groups of *vatos* check out the scene to scope out single *rucas*. Couples interlock their arms and stroll together towards the lobby of the theater. A nightingale whistle penetrates the air, and a shrieking sound is heard as shouts and yells fill the air. The doors of the theatre abruptly open as bodies spill out onto the boulevard pavement. A group of *vatos* line up tightly, and gestures and obscenities ring through the night air. *Rucas* hold onto their *vatos* to dissuade them from throwing blows. Flamboyant lowriders blaring Rick James inch by as squealing girls scream out in celebration.

Two *vatos* begin to push and shove each other against the theatre glass doors, and their *rucas* start to yell and scream at them to "Stop!" Some of the movie scenes are being played out for everyone to watch—no tickets needed. The crowd on the sidewalk began to encircle the disorderly moviegoers. Car horns, nightingale whistles, shouts, and "Suavecito" by Malo pulsate through the night air as the sidewalk drama takes flight. A siren mixes in with the beats of the night. Shouts from homies pierce the carousing. *Vatos* and *rucas* quickly evaporate like a hot breath on a chilly morning. Lowriders continue to flow down the boulevard blasting "Cowboys to Girls" by the Intruders, as their hydraulics zoom and swoosh to the beat of the music.

Dining While Mexican

Early Saturday morning we both bounded upon several buses going here, there, and eventually somewhere far away from home. Ultimately, we landed in a different world filled with trees, birds, and green grassy lanes. There were clean sidewalks, no smog, and fresh smelling air. *So this is where the good air lives*. Visions of food dragged us to this place. We could see our destination. We disembarked at the bus stop. Through large picture windows, we could see people enjoying platefuls of delectable and scrumptious breakfast goodies. Pancakes, sausage, bacon, eggs sunny-side up, hash browns, toast, orange juice, hot chocolate, and decaf coffee visions rolled around in our heads.

My mother and I enter an old-fashioned diner on the northeastern side of Los Angeles. The restaurant was bustling with customers and waitresses. The smell of breakfast wafted through the air like blooming flowers. Groups of people were enjoying abundant plates filled with ham omelets, French toast, carafes of orange juice and hot coffee. Elevator music played in the background which set a tone of relaxation.

We stepped in, and the sign read: SEAT YOURSELF. So we did. We had traveled so far, and so long our stomachs were aching for the mouthfuls of goodness on our plates. Other customers walked in and took their seats. The sounds of happy customers munching away filled the air. The waitresses walked in and out of the swinging doors where cooks bustled, and metal spatulas scraped the hot grill. Tables were bussed and wiped down all around. Still, other customers arrived and found open booths or tables by the large windows.

Minutes ticked and still no menus. No "Good morning" greetings. Busboys who looked like us, had their heads down and rushed past us, pulling carts filled with dirty plates, dirty glasses and half-eaten meals. My mother squirmed in her seat. I watched as waitresses strode quickly past us, holding large round trays filled to the rim with plates of food steaming out of the kitchen. We continued to wait.

Other customers received happy greetings and complimentary water or juice. Napkins rolled with silverware were brought in by busboys filling all the tables except ours. We glanced at the large black clock above the large seating counter ticking away, almost taunting us. My mother prompted me to speak up and call over a waitress, but my courage managed to stay under cover. I begged someone to notice with my eyes, but no one wanted to acknowledge us.

Frustration began to bubble in our chests. We had been in this situation before in other places. My mother started to mumble in Spanish and broken English about the service. I felt embarrassed. I didn't want a fight. I wanted to be accepted. I was hungry. She was hungry. My mother stood, grabbed her purse and spoke louder and said "*Vamonos*." She wanted us to get out of there. The feeling felt like a chokehold. We stood up, and the waitresses kept ignoring us, strolling past like if we were stinky dumpsters ready for pick up day.

The next moment we stood outside the diner as people sipping coffee, chomping on scrambled eggs and toast, peered at us like fish in an aquarium. Our stomachs felt empty, and they gurgled their disapproval. We had traveled all this way and had no food, just humiliation. We rode several buses back to our side of town. Breakfast time had ended, and we made our way to a Jack in the Box close to home. We bought tacos, small burgers, fries, and onion rings. There, everybody looked and talked like us. We could dine while Mexican.

'78 Walkout

The sound of the passing bell penetrated the afternoon calm as a stampede of feet stormed and poured out of buildings and onto the high school quad. High pitched screams and shouts erupted from the mouths of excited brown-skinned teenagers rushing past the blooming rose bushes, and edged lawn pathways toward the secured and massive black wrought iron school front gates. Beyond the gates, the neighborhood street pedestrian traffic was at a typical standstill and only the rush of the light street traffic droned on like spokes on a fan. The collection of student voices began to rise and fall and mix with the hum of the neighborhood, as the mass which evacuated the buildings approached the gates. The large steel chain which held the gates together were dislodged enough for bodies to spill out onto the front concrete steps. Cardboard signs displaying NO ON 13 mysteriously sprang up in the air like dandelions floating in the wind. Chicano students began to chant "Walkout! Walkout!" Only a decade ago the same scene had played out in the same place. Students had been fed up with the system that despised, ignored, and manipulated them, but they fought. Ten years later they rose up again like bubbles in a soda glass to defend what others had struggled to attain. Now those shadows of the past exploded onto the campus once again.

The school administrators with bullhorns in hand bellowed at the mob in the quad to get back to class. Car drivers honked and slinked down the street as they joined the students in their enthusiasm. The protesting students responded with arm and fist gestures like deranged orchestra conductors as they drizzled onto the pavement. The dean of students and vice principals repeatedly demanded the students' attention, but the crowd of bodies became deliberate in their intent to defy the authorities in their vigorous demonstration.

Earlier that morning the whispers and chatter about the protest had been set among the locker-lined corridors. The announcement spread like wildfire during the nutrition break among the students. Whispers and notes were passed in classrooms all around the school in preparation for the signal bell to ring and the onslaught to begin. The crowd of students outside the gate had grown exponentially across the expansive school façade like moss on a stone. The walkout was in full force as cars beeped at the mob of students which overwhelmed the sidewalk and began to encompass the schools' grassy walled mounds. Students chanted and others grinned— enjoying the break from class. Others laughed at the lookie-loos decelerating to take a quick glance at the frenzied sight. More cardboard signs flared-up among the students and bounced and bopped like daisies in an open field. Suddenly the school narcs in their detective suits paced among the protesting students and studied the crowd. The short Mexican principal with a bullhorn pressed firmly in hand and on his lips announced the consequences of their behavior if they refused to go back to class. Frustrated school officials and irritated teachers on break tried to corral pockets of students back inside. Others yelled and made traffic cop arm gestures to no avail. Eager students proclaimed their rights to gripe and reveled in their successful afternoon endeavor. The principal roared out more warnings and then suddenly lowered the bullhorn in frustration and tried to coax the crowd. He convinced some students to return to class. Other students still resisted the warnings and became staunch in their resolve. The students who did not comply would be dealt with swiftly by the principal who took mental notes. Some of the cardboard signs began to disappear as annoyed faces appeared on those earlier excited teenage expressions.

School busses became temporary barriers to the display of the walkout event on the school sidewalk. The busses stood curbside in preparation for after school boarding of students. Across the street, cars pulled in and out of the burger stand and by the corner liquor store people waited for the local bus. The release bell rang, which announced the day was over, and with that students rushed onto the street like a tsunami wave. Many joined the crowd on the steps, and eventually it became a swarm. The cardboard signs reappeared like an erupting nose pimple. The principal and other administration commanded the students to disperse and go home. Students stood around, aroused with the chanting and hand gestures. The traffic became heavier and louder as beeping and honking of cars joined in the jubilation of the youngsters. The protest took on a circus atmosphere as the school officials continued their warnings, but it was all for nothing.

The walkout had been planned and executed, and now the more significant event would take place. Students rushed together and walked down the street and across intersections and met others joining the protest. The mass spread and turned street corners and met others willing to march with them. They walked and walked until they were in a multitude, chanting, shouting and protesting. Down this street and that street – the students joined others to continue the same fight…that had started a decade earlier.

Invisible

Junior year…meeting with the high school counselor. *What will you be when you grow up?* Those words spin in my brain. "Be a bookkeeper like my wife," he recommends. The word bookkeeper bounces around my mind like balls whisking about in a bingo machine. I don't even like numbers. I want to go to law school. *Can you help me with that?* The question floats in and then out of my brain. The counselor seems to be having a conversation with himself. He goes on about how his wife likes being a part time bookkeeper.

My mind is screaming out, *what are you talking about?* He doesn't see me. He is moving papers around on his desk. He adds up numbers and writes something down. How come he doesn't ask me about what I want? I'm used to that. No one ever asks. I murmur under my breath as the counselor continues his motivational speech.

Wow. He keeps talking like I'm invisible. Maybe all of us who look like me are unseen. He shuffles paper around and examines my credits and looks at me as he probably looks at most of his other students assigned to him.

I stare at the wall behind him and see Army posters and old college banners. I ask him about colleges in general but he doesn't seem interested in giving any information. My brain shouts out "I want to go to Harvard!" *How do people go there?* I think about it but don't say anything to him. He doesn't care. Nobody does.

I dream the big dream. My mother says only rich people go to college. Only people that don't look like us go to college. We only know about hard work. We keep our heads down and work with our hands and backs. No one I know has gone to college. Who do I ask? My counselor wants me to graduate. Half our class has dropped out probably because half our senior class felt like I did. *No options for you!*

I stare back at him and wonder what should I do? He continues talking and staring at the paperwork and past me. Then he continues about credits and graduation and then that is it. Invisible me walks out the same way I did. No options. No information. No future? Well that is what you might think! I am invisible no more….

Rumors

Amelia left the other day. She jumped into a car with her trunk, backpack, and a jacket and sped off. She was so excited and nervous at the same time. Hours later she arrived at her destination. It was crazy. She was starting her new life. So many miles away from her old life. It all happened so fast. She made the decision, and POOF, she changed her life just like that.

The rumors started. *La gente* from the neighborhood looked out their windows when the brown-skinned girl left and shook their heads. They all wondered what would cause her to go in such a hurry. They didn't hear any argument from the mother. Nobody fought or got angry. In the following days, they saw Amelia's mother go to the store. Catch the bus downtown. They saw her water her plants and sweep her front steps.

At the corner grocery store, a neighbor stopped her mother and asked her about Amelia. She told the neighbor that her daughter had left for college. The letters c-o-l-l-e-g-e flipped a somersault in the neighbor's brain. Was Amelia's mother serious? Her daughter went to college. *Oh sure, that's the reason.* The neighbor quickly departed. The rumors flew like crows on a rampage.

One late afternoon the gossip sparked as firecrackers on the Fourth of July. The neighbors commented that the girl had run away. Others intimated she did not go to college—she was probably in jail. Some insisted she was pregnant and on the street. Others asserted she was a drug addict. Still, others attested she was selling herself on the streets. They all felt sorry for her mother. One of the neighbors concluded that none of their kids went to college and only *gringos* go to the university. No *mexicanos* get to go to college. Especially a poor Mexican girl. That would be ridiculous.

The neighbors felt sorry for Amelia's mother and wanted to comfort her and let her know how sorry they were for her troubles. One day her mother was walking to the neighborhood store, and a concerned neighbor stopped her. Amelia's mother heard the neighbor's concerns and was dumbstruck at their assertions of what had happened to her daughter. She interrupted the neighbor and walked away.

Amelia got back the other day. She jumped out of the car with her trunk, backpack, and a jacket and slammed the car door. She stood on the sidewalk in front of her house. She was excited and nervous at the same time. She had come home. It was crazy how your life changes in an instant. So many miles back to her old life. It all happened. College had been incredible, and now she had to figure out her next step.

The rumors started....

Love vs. Death

Twenty dollars pressed into the woman's expectant palm at the door and minutes later she explained I would soon die. She cautioned death would occur in a matter of a month. She nonchalantly revealed this as she methodically tucked the twenty dollars in her bosom, and then proceeded to turn each strange and colorful card I had previously selected over, upon a small round card table in the center of the room. I sat on a slouching couch chair, wide-eyed as the woman stared at me with dark bloodshot eyes, as she spewed a list of items I would need to fight death. The list began with candles, a couple of eggs, strands of hair, and ended with an article of clothing. I thought those things seemed simple enough to fight my demise. She murmured I would also need to make consecutive trips to a cemetery at midnight.

As the woman spoke, my mind spun the thread of her instructions into knots. She claimed the cards explained that he did not love me and I had only been a distraction because he had a real true love. This true love had set a spell of hate and wanted me dead.

However, she urged I could fight death and love with her help of course.

Did I want that kind of love? Was it that important? Her price tag of $500 dollars and a down payment of $150 by the next evening did not provide any solace. I instantly felt used by everyone concerned. He led me to this ridiculous decision to seek a con artist that preys on sadness and sorrow. He used me to satisfy some self-esteem issue. *Stupid, stupid, stupid...get yourself out of...all of it,* my mind screamed!! She reads my eyes and advises; I should take care of this quickly because death is coming for me. I shudder only slightly as the words slip out of her mouth succinctly and tersely like a snake shedding its skin.

I seemed to become more emboldened than afraid as I stare down at cards on the small coffee table. She quickly picks them up and shuffles them. *Well, unfortunately, death has indeed spoken.* She threatens she is correct in her advice because some card she picks out says so. Too bad I'm dead no matter what; unless I pay up and hang out with the dead. I stare back at those dark bloodshot eyes. I smile, and then slowly I rise and smirk. She frowns and explains that I don't have a lot of time to think about this. I turn and walk out the door. I think if death wants me I'm here waiting like everyone else...as for love...I'll be here waiting like everyone else....

Chicana Paradise

Like a dewdrop on a spider's web, the yellow smog hung upon the horizon of downtown Los Angeles in the distance. Her town was crisscrossed by the bustling Five Freeway and the iron and wooden tracks of the Pacific Railroad. The L.A. River, in its concrete burial vault, framed the town on one side, and on the other, the hills of Montecito Heights surrounded the original East L.A. neighborhood. The site where she first drew breath and toddled. The place that watched the dramas of life unfold. Moving from block to block, trying to run from a monster disguised as a man who bled red but had no heart and no soul. No one helped. No one cared. People just talked and threw stones. The neighborhood filled with sadness and tears.

There were sanctuaries from life's chaos which appeared erect and commanding in the neighborhood. One on Avenue 20, which gave her solace, caressed her heart and burned bright in her eyes. The flowers, the candles, and the angelic voices rose in her throat as she stared into the eyes of religious icons. On Sichel Street, a beautiful golden altar sparkled from the prayer votives emanating their pleas up to a life-size Jesus on the cross. The quietness gave her a respite from the whirlwind surrounding her.

Avenue 20, Daly, Workman, Main, Griffin, Broadway—names of avenues and streets that filled her with happiness as a child but with a dark undertone that only she knew to keep quiet. Each one of those streets had a place in her existence. Life, death, and occasional blissfulness occurred side by side upon those streets. Moving always in the same place with ties to those religious icons gave her some stability. She wanted quiet, and a place to rest but those things did not come so easy. The monster continued his attack, and she was the casualty. No one cared. No one helped. People just threw stones.

One day, running away ceased, and running forward began. Life and occasional happiness remained. The roar of the Five Freeway and the smog of Downtown L.A. became much denser and more yellowy in the distance. Her neighborhood was alive and humming with new dramas to unfold and dreams to catch. Her life had been filled with so much turmoil she was unsure of where to go. What was her path? No one really had an answer. There were those who wanted her to fit in like a puzzle piece. Find your place and stay there. She did not want that...or did she? That monster from the past had left his mark on her soul. She had no dreams for her future. She had no sense of what could be. She had to build them all by herself. She stumbled.

Her town was still there no matter what had happened and no matter how ugly she had felt. It was her paradise—a place of her own resurrection. She would find bliss under her memories. Those would sustain her. The neighborhood that was an eyewitness to her sorrows did not disown her. She became stronger and more determined to construct a life that made sense to her. The marks left from her past began to fade away but were not forgotten. They were always a reminder of who she was and what she could be. She persevered.

She was molded by her neighborhood. It was imperfect, tough, direct, real, Mexican, spiritual, dangerous, in your face, and poignant. She was all those things. She felt all of them when she was there. She was unsure if she would leave one day because those memories grabbed and held on so tight that letting go felt impolite. The town that gave her so much. One day a spark of light entered her mind and stirred her spirit. She would begin a journey. She would carry her Chicana paradise in her heart forever.

I'm Tired Since, I Was a Very Young Child

I'm tired
since I was a very young child,
I was bullied because of my gender.
You're a girl you have nothing to say,
Keep your head down and go away.

I was discriminated against because of my culture,
You're a Mexican-American you don't belong here or there,
Whites hated me, and Mexicans shunned me.

I was made to feel different because I was poor,
You have nothing; You are nothing,
You are less than; You will never be more.

I was called a "bastard child"
because I was raised in a single-parent home,
You are less and unwanted,
You must be defective.

I'm tired
since I was a very young child,
my intelligence was questioned,
my high IQ was tested and ridiculed,
because it was unbelievable,
How could intelligence grow out of poverty?
I was not encouraged to be successful because of my
brown skin.

You will never amount to much; your kind never do.

I was told I was ugly and skinny; no one wants you,
My self-confidence was attacked; my physical
appearance was dissected
It didn't match what others expected.

I'm tired
since I was a very young child,
I have fought the battles of prejudice, discrimination,
and injustice;
being singled out, isolated, and ostracized.

All my life,
They, those, them pounded those insecurities into my
soul,
They scarred my heart.

I'm tired no more,
I found it was not me; it was them; their ignorance
and beliefs,
I am proud of who and what I am.
No one can deny my gender, my culture, my
presence, my beauty, and my truth.
I have battled back using my many strengths; being
resilient and intelligent.
I am who I am, and no force can touch my existence,
    I Am Tired No More.

Epilogue

A Mother's Passing

She lay motionlessly on an old wood framed bed; her face still displayed the shadow of a young woman with delicate features and a silky crown of curly auburn hair. Her sallow face had thinned from the malnutrition and her droopy hazel eyes contrasted against the dark shadows that hung low against her high cheekbones. She was the mother of five surviving children; one had died at birth. Two young girls slumbered peacefully across from the fireplace.

The fire crackled, popped, and danced across the mantle wall as the family slept in their one-room adobe home. The summer storm bounced above them on the old tin roof to its rhythmical beat. The two young girls snoozed in an old single metal cot. The large wooden front door reverberated with each thunder strike and angry rumble in the distant sky. The darkness peered through a small square wavy glass window nestled high up in the rear of the room.

Short, breathless gasps fogged the oxygen mask as the oxygen tank "shhhh" sound filled the darkened room. Her exhaustive moans escaped, while air filtering through the oxygen mask spewed from the tank next to her bed. Her arms flailed and swung around her head involuntarily due to the powerful medication that she was under. Her body was determined not to release her from the agony of the final deep sleep. Her delicate features and silky crown of white hair and sallow face had thinned from the lack of food and her semi-opened dilated drugged hazel eyes contrasted against the dark shadows that hung low against her high cheekbones. She was the mother of one surviving child: three had died at birth. Her only daughter and grandson sat on either side holding her hands, soothing her with gentle weeping whispers of love.

Television chatter filled the assisted living hallway outside the room. Nurses pushed medicine carts and made their rounds as phantom patients slowly rolled their wheelchairs or pushed walkers past the room entrance. The constant "shhhh" from tank marked the time as her grandson and daughter's eyes filled with tears and streamed down their cheeks. A nurse walked into to check and make a note of the event. She stated that the end was near and the flailing would end and calmness would soon appear. The elderly women's body would subside to the medication. The fight would end. Beyond, in other rooms, in other beds, other suffering bodies moaned and ached in unison.

The rainstorm pounded the ground outside the adobe house. Mud puddles sprayed against the wire-fenced posts. The water drenched the tin roof which poured down streams upon the damp earth. One of the girls with a crown of auburn hair awoke to the sound of a far-off train whistle. She rubbed her hazel eyes with her little fist. She stared at the fire and then turned around and saw mama's sallow face and half-closed hazel eyes in the flickering of the flame light. The little girl sat up. Her bare feet dangled above the dirt floor. She slipped down and tiptoed across the cold earthen floor as the rain hammered the front doorstep outside.

The girl's small form cast a ghostly shadow upon the worn and tattered serape blanket tucked neatly under her mother's thin arms. Her mother's breathing was shallow, and her droopy eyes seemed stuck in a faraway place. The young girl's auburn curly hair fell upon her high cheekbones. She took her small index finger from her right hand and gently traced her mother's delicate facial features which resembled her own. Her mother had been frail and in bed for many days. Their father had abandoned the family – now only their older siblings would check on their mother. The little girl had listened to the grown-up conversations, and she knew her mother was sick. The little girl moved her hand and stroked her mother's curly-hair ringlets. The storm continued to slam down on the home, and the young girl raised her face to stare at the large wooden cross dangling from the black beaded rosary on the bed's metal headboard. She prayed to La Virgen and Jesus as her mother had taught her.

The flailing and oxygen sound slowed down. The old woman's breathing became short gasps of air. Her arms twitched, and her eyes fluttered as if she wanted to break free to see. Her eyes went cross; her head moved side to side. It seems she could still hear them; she tried to speak. Her daughter held her hand and gently stroked her hair and arm. Her grandson held her other hand and soothingly spoke to her. They both were in silent grief and agony as tears continued to stream down their cheeks. They stared back and forth at each other and this old woman who had cared for them as they had cared for her now in her declining years. She had watched, protected, and loved them both, as they both cared, protected, and loved her in return.

The nurse returned to check once again and take note. She pointed out that the old woman was nearing the final moments. Death was coming close. The old woman's hands were getting colder by the second. Her hair and face were beginning to turn pale blue-gray. Everything was in slow motion now. The oxygen slowed. The gasps shortened. Her eyes fluttered and closed. Her hands were frozen, and she slipped away like a cool breeze on a warm spring day. Her grandson and daughter wept and held each other. They kissed her goodbye realizing that she was gone.

The little girl stared at her mother and looked up at the curved glass where she saw a speck of light peering through. She tiptoed towards the fireplace and stirred the cooling embers as her mother had done many times before. She wrapped her ten little fingers around some small pieces of firewood and threw them in. Slowly a small flame began to flicker gently. The little girl tiptoed back to her mother's bedside. She touched her mother's fingertips and felt sleepiness creep upon her eyelids, so she returned to the metal cot. Her sister was gently breathing on her side. She slipped into the bed without a sound.

The morning brought the crow of a rooster and hens clucking about outside. The little girl woke up as her sister lay still, sleeping soundly next to her. She stepped lightly towards her mother who had not moved one inch. The little girl gently touched her mother and noticed how cold her skin seemed. She looked at her mother's face it was pale and almost translucent. She did not hear her breathing anymore. She caressed her mother's auburn hair which had become darker overnight. The next moment she heard voices and footsteps coming towards the front door. She heard one of her elder sisters calling her name to open the door. She went over to the door and pulled a piece of wood which had secured the lock. Her sister and her husband walked in. Her little sister woke up and then the rest of the family arrived and was now surrounding her mother. For many hours later, the tiny adobe house was filled with tears and sorrow. Her mother was dead.

A mother's passing.

About the Author

Born and raised in a neighborhood northeast of Los Angeles, California, Jesi Lopez Malignaggi holds a Bachelor of Arts in English Education and a Master of Arts in English Literature. She is an educator.

Made in the USA
Las Vegas, NV
24 March 2022

46241024R00074